GREAT MOMENTS IN SPORTS

MICHAEL J. PELLOWSKI

Illustrated by Myron Miller

Sterling Publishing Co., Inc.
New York

DEDICATION

Life is the only game where how you perform
is really important . . . because God is the
referee.

M.J.P

To Michael Morgan Pellowski

Edited by Claire Bazinet

Library of Congress Cataloging-in-Publication Data

Pellowski, Michael.
    Not-so-great moments in sports / Michael J. Pellowski :
illustrated by Myron Miller.
        p.   cm.
    Includes index.
    ISBN 0-8069-1256-1
    1. Sports—Humor.   2. Sports—Anecdotes.   I. Title.
GV707.P45   1994
08-04-94—dc20   94-30974
                                                         CIP

10   9   8   7   6   5   4   3   2   1

First paperback edition published in 1995 by
Sterling Publishing Company, Inc.
387 Park Avenue South, New York, N.Y. 10016
© 1994 by Michael J. Pellowski
Distributed in Canada by Sterling Publishing
% Canadian Manda Group, One Atlantic Avenue, Suite 105
Toronto, Ontario, Canada M6K 3E7
Distributed in Great Britain and Europe by Cassell PLC
Wellington House, 125 Strand, London WC2R 0BB, England
Distributed in Australia by Capricorn Link (Australia) Pty Ltd.
P.O. Box 6651, Baulkham Hills, Business Centre, NSW 2153, Australia
Manufactured in the United States of America

Sterling ISBN 0-8069-1256-1 Trade
            0-8069-1257-X Paper

Contents

Hoop Blahs!

Game Player

Lionel Simmons of the Sacramento Kings suffered an odd injury during the 1990–91 NBA season. Simmons was plagued by wrist and forearm tendonitis that year, which caused him to miss two professional basketball games. The funny thing is, Simmons didn't injure himself on the basketball court. He hurt himself by playing too much Nintendo Game Boy.

Uniform Insanity

The Liberty Basketball Association, which is a women's professional league, attempted to dress up its players in something new for the 1990–91 season. A "unitard" was designed to be worn by players in the league. The new uniform was made of an elastic, form-fitting material. However, the original design of the unitard turned out to be so revealing that it later had to be greatly modified so that fans would concentrate more on the game and less on the players.

Boring

Believe it or not, in a game between the Fighting Irish of Notre Dame and the Wildcats of Kentucky in 1982, Irish players made 213 passes while holding the ball before anyone took a single shot. All of that passing didn't help much, as Notre Dame ended up losing to Kentucky 34 to 28 in overtime.

The Wild One

In 1993 Coach Don Nelson of the Golden State Warriors found an interesting way to escape the pressures of professional basketball. Nelson relaxed by riding his motorcycle with a group of biker friends known as "Nell's Angels."

The Naked Truth

In 1982, two high school basketball coaches in Oregon came up with a new way to practise free throws. The coaches allowed boys on the Santiam High School basketball squad to hold a strip, free-throw shooting contest during practice in the high school gym to help the team combat its midseason blahs. The idea of the one-time event was to liven things up for the team at practice. The free-throw strip-off certainly did that. Several members of the Junior Varsity squad ended up wearing nothing but socks and sneakers by the time the contest ended. Unfortunately for the losers, members of the school's cheerleading squad showed up and caught them out of uniform. The two coaches who allowed the contest to take place were later formally reprimanded by local school board officials.

Winning Isn't Everything

Every sports buff knows you can't win them all. However, it is nice to win one occasionally. Unfortunately, the NBA's Dallas Mavericks had a tough time notching a single victory during a 20-game period in 1993. The Mavericks tied a single-season NBA record for futility that year by losing twenty games in a row. However, they managed to top the Minnesota Timberwolves by a score of 93–89 before they eclipsed the dreadful 20-straight loss mark set by the Philadelphia 76ers in 1972–73.

As bad as the Mavericks and 76ers had to be to lose twenty straight they were still better than the hapless Cleveland Cavaliers who set an all-time NBA record for consecutive losses. The Cavaliers once dropped 24 straight games, a losing streak that spanned two seasons (1981–82 and 1982–83).

Years of Tears

The boys' basketball team of Manchester Memorial High School in New Hampshire learned to live with losing in the 1990s. The team went two and a half years without a single victory on the court, chalking up an 0–56 record, counting tournament games.

As bad as the Manchester Memorial record sounds, it's not even close to the painful losing streak of the Carbondale Sacred Heart girls' basketball team in Pennsylvania. Carbondale Sacred Heart, a girls' prep school, lost 141 straight games during the 1980s.

Taking a Licking

Some losses are harder to swallow than others. When two girls' basketball teams from Ohio faced off in December of 1993, the result was a lopsided loss that could choke a horse. Licking Heights High School started fast out of the scoring gate and led 32–0 over Columbus Liberty Christian High School after one quarter. The score at the conclusion of the half was 52–0 in favor of Licking Heights. In the third quarter Columbus Liberty Christian ended the shutout and scored what proved to be its only basket of the game. Licking Heights High School went on to capture a 102–2 victory over Columbus Liberty Christian High School.

Getting Trashed

When the Rutgers Scarlet Knights upset the West Virginia Mountaineers at home in February of 1992 and ended the Mountaineers' 10-game winning streak, the hometown crowd didn't appreciate the visitors' performance. As the Rutgers players exited the court and passed the Mountaineers' student section, the Scarlet Knights were bombarded with bits of garbage, pieces of candy, and even paper cups filled with tobacco juice. The angry crowd didn't just talk trash to the victorious visitors, they threw it at them. Officials from West Virginia later apologized for the incident.

A Wrong Bomb

When West Virginia visited Olean, New York, in March of 1993 to play St. Bonaventure, the fans at courtside expected to see a few long bombs made in the contest. The matchup between the two schools turned into a real dud when a bomb scare was phoned in to Reilly Arena while the game was being played. Security personnel quickly evacuated the teams and some 3,200 other people in the arena, forcing them all to wait outside in a driving snowstorm for about thirty minutes while the security staff searched the arena. After it was determined that there was no bomb anywhere in the building the game resumed. The West Virginia team was unaffected by the delay due to the bomb scare and exploded for a 82–67 victory over the St. Bonaventure squad.

Fallen Arches

The experts knew Orlando Magic superstar Shaquille O'Neal had the scoring ability to break a game open when he entered the NBA in 1993. The 300-pound rookie managed to break something that astonished even the experts when Orlando travelled to New Jersey to play the Nets at the Meadowlands Arena in April of 1993. In the first period of play Shaquille took a pass under the board and spun around the Nets' Derrick Coleman and Dwayne Schintzius. As O'Neal went up to slam the ball through the hoop, Schintzius fouled Shaquille, forcing him to hang on the rim to keep from falling. What did fall was the entire backboard, as the huge Orlando rookie broke the backboard's hydraulic support system. Down came the rim, the backboard, and the three-foot-tall shot clock which was mounted atop the backboard. O'Neal barely escaped being hit on the head by the clock as everything landed with a thud. The game was halted and delayed for fifty minutes as crews worked to repair the damage done by the amazing Shaquille O'Neal, a true NBA game breaker!

Gag Gift

Player Bob McAdoo received a thoughtless gift from the New Jersey Nets on Christmas Eve, 1981. McAdoo was axed from the Nets the day before Christmas.

Kelvin Upshaw fared even worse than Bob McAdoo during holiday seasons over the years. Upshaw was sent packing from the Boston Celtics team on Christmas Eve, 1989, and a year later dropped from the Dallas Mavericks roster on Christmas Eve, 1990.

Bad Luck

Mike Mitchell was very upset when his Gold Coast Rollers team lost a game to the Illawarra Hawks in the Australian National Basketball League in May of 1992. Mitchell was so mad that he smashed his fist through a glass-wire panel in his team's locker room door after storming off the court following the loss. The cut on his arm that resulted from his display of anger needed surgery to repair.

Seams Bad

Chuck Daly is known for being a snazzy dresser. Once, while coaching the Detroit Pistons in an NBA game, Chuck angrily leaped off of the bench to vehemently protest a foul called on one of his Piston players. Daly's expensive tailored suit slacks couldn't stand the strain of his wild gyrations and ripped apart at the rear seam, exposing his underwear for everyone to see. Chuck Daly knew his shorts were showing and didn't care. He continued to coach in his ripped pants for the remaining five minutes or so of the game.

Thanksgiving Turkey

Howie Dallmar, a player for the old Philadelphia Warriors, didn't turn in much of a shooting exhibition against the New York Knicks on Thanksgiving Day, 1947. Dallmar took fifteen shots in the contest, and missed every one of them.

Daddy's Boy

Every basketball fan knows that Bobby Knight, the super-successful coach at Indiana, is hot-tempered. On December 9, 1993, Bobby was suspended from coaching for one game for losing his cool after one of his players made an errant pass while playing against Notre Dame. In fact, the player Bobby Knight blew up at was his own son, Patrick Knight, who played for his dad on the Indiana squad.

The following day after Coach Knight's suspension was announced, Indiana took on Tennessee Tech in a basketball game at Bloomington, Indiana. Of course, all Coach Bobby Knight could do while he was suspended was stand on the sidelines and watch.

What he saw was his son, Patrick, get in a scuffle with Greg Bibb of Tennessee Tech in the second half. Officials quickly tossed Pat Knight and Greg Bibb out of the contest for losing their tempers. Hot-tempered Patrick Knight then joined his father, hot-tempered Bobby Knight, on the sidelines for the rest of the game, which Indiana won 117–73.

Obedience Schooled

Kenny Smith, who played for the Houston Rockets in the NBA in 1992, was always a very coachable player. Years ago, when Smith was just ten years old, he was handling the ball in a youth basketball contest that his team was winning with only seconds to play. Kenny's coach didn't want to risk turning the ball over to the opposition, so he yelled out for Kenny Smith to "sit on the ball," or not take a shot. Since Kenny Smith was taught never to disobey his coach, he promptly put the ball on the floor and actually sat on it until time expired.

Foul Deed

The women's basketball team of Rutgers-Camden lost a game to New Jersey rival Rutgers-Newark in December of 1991 even though Rutgers-Camden was leading by two points in the second overtime period. The odd loss occurred because Rutgers-Camden, which started the game with only seven players on its squad, watched in horror as six of those players eventually fouled out of the contest. Since Rutgers-Camden couldn't finish the game with only one player on the court, Rutgers-Newark won the contest by forfeit.

Huddle Befuddlement

University of Miami coach Leonard Hamilton used a time-out to talk to his team with sixteen seconds left in the Hurricanes' court contest against the University of Pittsburgh Panthers on January 24, 1993. At the time the Hurricanes were leading in the game by a basket. Coach Hamilton was so intent on making his squad understand his last-second instructions to preserve a victory that he kept his team on the sidelines even after the scoreboard horn had sounded twice to signal the time-out was over.

Since the officials had no obligation to wait for the Hurricanes to get back into position on the court, they turned the ball over to the team that had possession of it last. The team that had the ball and got it back was Pittsburgh. The Panthers quickly inbounded the ball while the nearest Miami defender was still sixty feet away, and promptly went in for an uncontested lay-up to knot the game at 84 points apiece. Miami then rushed back onto the court, but the damage had already been done. Seconds later a Pittsburgh player stole the ball from a still confused Miami player and the Panthers scored again, to steal a win from a Hurricane team that had blown a chance to ice a victory because it had been late breaking from the huddle after a time-out.

No Job Security

Even though Chuck Daly signed a three-year contract when he became head coach of the Cleveland Cavaliers in 1981, he wasn't completely sure the job would last. Instead of setting down roots near his new workplace, he decided to keep living in a rented motel room for a while. Daly apparently made a wise decision, as he ended up getting axed after just 93 days on the job.

Wash Out

When you're playing a basketball game and raindrops keep falling on your head, it's time for officials to call the game a washout. That's just what happened on January 29, 1990, when Whippany Park High School met New Providence High School in a girls' basketball game in New Jersey. The game was played during a driving rainstorm which caused rainwater to build up on the roof of the Whippany Park gymnasium. The water on the roof began to leak through to the court below. The indoor raindrops were so bad, officials decided to postpone the contest until a drier date.

Foul Finish

Franklin High School and Colonia High School locked horns in a well-played tug-of-war for the Central New Jersey Group Three boys' basketball state title in March of 1994. With eleven seconds remaining in the contest, the score was tied and the ball belonged to Franklin. The Franklin five frantically pushed the ball down-court and hurriedly hit a three-point bucket to take the lead. Since Colonia had no time-outs and couldn't stop the clock from running out, the Franklin team began to celebrate capturing its first-ever state basketball title. Just then something bizarre happened to quiet the would-be victors. The officials signalled that the game wasn't over, even though no time was remaining on the clock.

In the madness that followed the last-chance Franklin shot, an assistant coach had accidentally dropped his clipboard in the playing area of the basketball court. The basketball officials ruled that dropping the clipboard on the court was "interference." They, therefore, put four seconds back on the clock and gave the ball to Colonia. A Colonia player then got off a shot, at the last tick of the four seconds, which was good and once again tied the game. The two teams were forced to play an overtime period. Colonia ended up winning the state championship 55 to 51 over a stunned Franklin squad. A clipboard had cost the Franklin squad the championship.

Foe Gotten

Prairie View A. & M. was ready to play a men's basketball contest against its rival, Texas College, in December of 1990. There was only one big problem: the Texas College basketball team never showed up for the game. A call to Texas College revealed that there had been a goof up: Prairie View A. & M. officials had never actually scheduled the court contest with its rival school.

Court Case

Jerry West was a star player for the Los Angeles Lakers for many years. In 1992, West was working as the General Manager of the Lakers. Arriving at the L.A. Forum parking lot on August 3, 1992, Jerry left his car and headed for the team offices. On the way he was held up by men who robbed him of his wallet and his 1985 NBA Championship Ring.

Car Sick

Head coach Kevin Loughery of the New Jersey Nets was noticeably absent as his team prepared to take on the Milwaukee Bucks on December 17, 1980. No one seemed to know where the Nets' head coach was or why he wasn't on hand for his team's home game.

When the game started the Nets still were without their main mentor, and assistant coach Bob MacKinnon was pressed into service to guide the New Jersey squad. Finally, with a little over six minutes remaining in the first half, a tardy Kevin Loughery showed up at his team's game. The late but irate coach of the Nets had gotten caught in a mammoth traffic jam on the Garden State Parkway while driving to the Nets game.

Cool Fan Support

When Manchester Memorial High School of New Hampshire took on Keene High School in a holiday basketball tournament in 1993, Manchester Memorial didn't receive much fan support from its student body. Only three students showed up to cheer their team on in what turned out to be a losing cause.

Unlisted Numbers

Hunter College in New York City got a wrong number when their new white basketball uniforms arrived at the start of the 1979 season. The basketball jerseys didn't have any numbers on them, they were all completely blank!

Cheers and Jeers

College basketball officials know when and how to put a stop to any verbal abuse they receive on the court. Occasionally a basketball coach or player will get out of hand and have to be tossed out of the game by an official.

In January of 1993, official Tom Higgins was in Philadelphia working a home game of St. Joseph's College when he was faced with a unique problem. After a player on the visiting team made a lay-up and crashed into the St. Joe's cheerleaders, who were sitting under the basket, a male cheerleader lost his temper. The cheerleader got into a dispute with official Tom Higgins and absolutely refused to quiet or calm down. Finally Tom Higgins decided to take control of the situation. The official tossed the St. Joe's cheerleader out of the game with nine minutes and forty-one seconds remaining to play in the first half.

Weird World of Sports

Deep Trouble

The 130th boat race between Oxford and Cambridge, annually held on the Thames River, got off to a slow start in March of 1984. In fact, the start of the race actually had to be postponed for a day because of an odd mishap.

The Cambridge crew was out on the water for a practice run about twenty minutes before the start of the big race when it accidentally smashed into the mooring rope of a stationary tug. The fluke accident tore away the bow section of the Cambridge boat and sent the oarsmen sailing overboard. Luckily no one was hurt and a replacement boat was available. It was the only time in the long history of the race that a boat had ever been wrecked while *preparing* for the race.

Top Side

All eyes were on a Danish oarswoman as she weighed in at the 1984 World Rowing Championships held at Nottingham, England. Brigidda Hamel received so much attention because, much to the embarrassment of the event's officials, Brigidda weighed in topless!

Whatever Suits You

The performance of the East German swim team was a big disappointment at the 1972 Olympic Games. The team did not win a single medal. When the East Germans showed up at the 1973 World Aquatic Championships a year later, the team appeared to have gone through a startling change. The biggest change was the style of swimwear worn by the East Germans. East Germany's swimmers had on suits of skin-tight, elastic, semi-see-through fabric that shocked everyone at the championships held at Belgrade, Yugoslavia.

The attire of the East Germans really raised a big commotion among the competition. Teams from other countries thought the tight and revealing suits were totally inappropriate athletic wear. Ignoring the complaints and rude comments, the East Germans went on to capture ten of the fourteen possible Gold Medals at the 1973 World Aquatic Championships.

Shortly after the amazing triumph of the East Germans, other swim teams around the world quickly began wearing the same type of suits they had previously condemned.

Water Bed

Twelve-year-old Kevin Anderson of South Africa attempted to swim the English Channel in 1980 but didn't make it. The young swimmer became so exhausted while swimming that he fell asleep in the water and had to be pulled into the safety of the boat following him. However, Kevin did manage to stay awake and swim the Channel during a second attempt later in the same year.

A Fishy Tale

Quatrain, a champion South African thoroughbred, had to be scratched from several races in July of 1980 for a very fishy reason. While exercising at a local beach that year the filly was taken into the ocean for a relaxing swim. Unfortunately for Quatrain, her fun romp in the sun came to a painfully quick end when a shark suddenly swam up and bit the horse on her left hind leg. After the wounded racehorse splashed out of the surf, it took twelve stitches to close the wound made by the shark's teeth.

Smashing Show

A crystal trophy is awarded to the winner of the Professional Bowling Association's U.S. Open Tournament. In 1991, the awarding of that trophy wasn't exactly the kind of smashing success tournament officials had hoped for. During the awards presentation, which took place on a live national television broadcast, the crystal top of the trophy somehow fell off of its stand and smashed into pieces on the floor.

Belly Flop!

A Turkish swimmer named Ersin Aydin once tried to set an endurance record by swimming down the Strait of Bosporus, which connects the Black Sea and the Sea of Marmara. Aydin spent 43 hours and 20 minutes in the water, which really wasn't a record. However, the amount of food consumed by the hungry Turk while in the water may have set a silly record of some kind. Ersin Aydin managed to consume 14 steaks, 20 cheese and meat sandwiches, 12 chocolate bars, 8 pounds of peaches, 25 glasses of tea, 10 bottles of fruit juice, and he topped it all off with 4 jars of honey. Aydin may not have been a great swimmer, but he sure had the stomach for competition.

An Honest Score

In the 1980s, top gymnast Philip Delesalle was unhappy with the score he received for his performance on the pommel horse at the Canadian National Championships. The strange thing was that Delesalle's score was a perfect 10. Philip honestly believed, however, that his performance wasn't good enough to rate that high a mark. So, after a chat with the judges, Philip Delesalle's score in the event was changed to 9.85, which made the Canadian gymnast much happier.

Sick of the Competition

Skaters Peter and Kitty Caruthers of the United States were big favorites to win the pairs competition at the Skate America Figure Skating Competition held at Lake Placid in 1982. Unfortunately for Peter and Kitty, the pair had to drop out of the competition at the last minute because Kitty was unexpectedly struck down by a truly "fowl" twist of fate. Kitty Caruthers couldn't skate because she came down with a bad case of the chicken pox.

Please, Don't Get the Point

Soviet fencer Vladimir Lapitsky really got the point made by his competitor, Adam Robak of Poland, while fencing in the Olympic Foil Team event held at Moscow in July of 1980. Lapitsky, a former world champion, was accidentally run through by Robak's weapon when the Polish fencer's foil broke against the side of Vladimir's mask and pierced the Russian's protective clothing. Luckily for Vladimir Lapitsky, the wound wasn't too serious and he later recovered from the freak accident.

Skiing's Last Resort

The Massachusetts High School State Cross Country Skiing Championships were held at an interesting site in 1989, 1990, and 1991. The Massachusetts Championship races were held in the state of Vermont! The skiing events had to be moved from the Bay State to the Green Mountain State because of a lack of snow in Massachusetts during those years.

Icing Call

If any athlete should know how to stand up on ice it should be a hockey player, right? Wrong! Take the case of Russian hockey goalie Vladislav Tretiak. In 1981, Tretiak was forced to stop playing in the U.S.S.R. National Hockey Championships after he stepped off a bus in Gorky (a city 250 miles east of Moscow), slipped on a patch of ice, and ended up fracturing his leg.

Cool Call

In January of 1992 an ice hockey game between the Vancouver Canucks and the Tampa Bay Lightning at Vancouver, British Columbia, had to be postponed because of Mother Nature. A heavy snowstorm that produced blizzard conditions caused the ice hockey game to be snowed out.

Vicious Cycle

Cyclist Betsy Tanner finished first at a 24-hour bicycle race held in New York's Central Park in 1980. However, Betsy, who logged 340 miles around the event's five-mile course, was almost prevented from receiving her first-place gold medal for an odd reason. Cyclists who participated in the race wore aprons which were stamped every time they sped past a checkpoint, to keep track of their completed laps. Betsy raced by the checkpoint at such a high rate of speed several times that the checker missed her apron and stamped the back of Betsy's T-shirt instead. When a judge noticed Betsy Tanner's apron was minus eight stamp marks she was almost awarded second place. To salvage the win and the first-place finish, Betsy showed her stamped T-shirt to the judges, who then awarded her the gold medal she deserved.

Whoops!

Chris Jordan thought he had won a 27-mile bike race in California in March of 1982 and eased up to celebrate his victory. Unfortunately Jordan mistakenly slowed down ten yards shy of the finish line, which allowed Shawn Storm to speed by him and steal first place.

Made in Japan, or America?

Sumo wrestling is the national sport of Japan. It is an ancient sport with many traditions. One tradition is the crowning of a Yokozuna, or Grand Champion, which is the highest rank a sumo wrestler can ever achieve. In 1993, for the first time in the long history of sumo wresting, a foreigner was awarded the rank of Yokozuna, besting the Japanese athletes at their own game. Chad Rowan, a six-foot eight-inch, 455-pound American from Hawaii (known in Japan by the wrestling name of Akebono) earned the rank of Grand Champion and became Yokozuna by winning the 15-day New Year's Grand Tournament in Tokyo.

Mementos

In November of 1993 one of the strangest sports mementos in history was purchased at a New York City auction by an unidentified fan. The memento was a package of five Champ condoms produced in the 1950s, one of which had a picture of baseball star Ted Williams on it. The odd sports memento sold for a bid of $165.00.

Captive Audience

Monticello Raceway publicity director Andy Furman had what he thought was a good idea for a publicity stunt in 1980. He proposed to let in to the track, free of charge, any local prison inmates who showed up at the track's opening night on May 1st. Furman's proposal for a night out at the track for anyone serving time in prison was quickly given a death sentence by local prison officials, who refused to cooperate with his liberal offer.

Don't Go Scratch

When the racehorse Thriver, ridden by top jockey Angel Cordero, was scratched from a race at New Jersey's Meadowlands track only moments before its start in 1980, bettors went wild. To prevent a possible riot over the incident, anxious track officials decided to refund more than $80,000 in wagers which had been placed on Thriver. The refund calmed the angry crowd and everyone went home happy.

Holiday Gift Horse

At a race at New Jersey's Freehold Raceway in 1990, a horse named Chanuka finished third just in front of another horse appropriately named Thenitebeforexmas.

Sometimes Losers Win

Even the losers were winners at Louisville Downs Race Track on March 17, 1981. When the track accidentally posted the wrong winning combination for the third-race perfecta, a lot of bettors at the track became lucky winners. The track officials posted 2–4 as the official results even though the correct order of finish was actually 2–1. To make up for its own mistake, the track generously agreed to pay off on both combinations, which made winners out of a lot of losers.

Not-So-Grand National

The Grand National Steeplechase was run at Aintree in Liverpool in 1993, but it really wasn't a race. Officially the 1993 Grand National never happened, even though more than 115 million dollars was wagered on the outcome of England's most famous horse race and several horses actually did complete the difficult and sometimes deadly course.

The Debate of the 1993 Grand National began when the race was originally held up by an animal rights demonstration concerned about the frequent spills horses take while running in steeplechase races. When the demonstration ended, a false start halted the field of forty horses after some mounts had covered about 300 yards. The horses were quickly returned to the starting line (starting gates are not used in steeplechase races) for a fresh start. Unfortunately, before the race could be started again in the correct manner, there was a second false start. Nine riders noticed the red flag that signalled another false start and remained at the line. The rest of the riders and horses broke from the start and were off! Several riders never realized the second start was false and rode their mounts all the way to the finish line even though the race wasn't officially on. Since a third start of the race was out of the question, the 1993 Grand National had to be declared void. There were no winners of the race's $150,000 in prize money and the over 115 million dollars wagered on the race by bettors had to be returned.

This Horse Gets the Nod

A horse named Lost Link must have been really tired as it waited in the starting gate at Saratoga Park in July of 1991. Lost Link fell asleep in the gate and had to be rudely awakened before the race began.

You're Not Finished

Jockey Kent Desormeaux made a crucial goof while riding Kotashaan at the Japan Cup at Fuchu, Japan, in November of 1993. Kotashaan was at the front of the pack and looked to have a chance for victory when Desormeaux mistook the 100-metre mark for the finish line and stood up in the saddle. Kotashaan instantly slowed down and was quickly passed by Legacy World, which won the race in front of Kotashaan to capture the 1.56 million winner's share of the race's purse.

Reverse Decision

Stock car driver Alan Kulwicki won the 1992 Winston Cup Driving Championship. Kulwicki celebrated capturing the title by taking a victory lap at Atlanta Motor Speedway while driving his racing car in reverse!

Wheel of Misfortune

Auto racer Jacques Dagat of France had a bit of bad luck at Monte Carlo in January of 1981. Dagat was in Monaco to drive his car in the Monte Carlo Auto Rally. He woke up on the eve of the race and went outside to find that the car he'd planned to drive in the rally had been stolen. Despite a search by police and an appeal broadcast over the radio for the return of Dagat's car, the automobile was not found in time for Jacques Dagat to compete in the 1981 Monte Carlo rally.

We Will Rock You

In 1980 the Himalayan Auto Rally, India's first international car rally, ended with no one ever reaching the finish line. Angry demonstrators, protesting the waste of precious gasoline for a race in a country where most people are too poor to own bicycles, cooked up a way to stonewall the wasteful rally. As the cars entered in the race drove through India's countryside, protestors hurled rocks and stones at the expensive autos. The stoning, which scarred and scratched the rally cars, continued until the race was declared officially over to protect the drivers and their cars from further bombardment. Shekhar Mehta of Kenya, in an Opel Ascoma, was named the winner of the odd race that ended before a single car crossed the finish line.

Inching Into a Higher Income Bracket

Ukrainian pole-vault star Sergei Bubka had a lot of record-setting vaults during the 1990–91 season. Bubka, a wise businessman, had a clause written into his contract with a shoe company that called for him to earn a bonus each and every time he bested the indoor and/or outdoor pole-vault records. Sergei managed to eclipse the old records eight times that season. Strangely enough, each time he upped the old records he bested them by about a mere quarter of an inch. Draw your own conclusions.

Heads Up!

Being a high-school track coach can be a real pain. Coach Marlow Gundmundsen of Lincoln Junior High School in California found that out in 1981. Gundmundsen was accidentally hit right on the noggin by an 8-pound shot thrown by one of his athletes. Luckily Coach Gundmundsen wasn't seriously hurt and only ended up with a pounding headache.

Young at Heart

Britain's Bob Wiseman didn't care that the computer recording racers' finish times was already shut off when he finished running in the first London Marathon, which was held in 1981. Wiseman knew his time of six hours plus wasn't exactly a record pace. Bob was just proud to finish. After all, he was 78 years old when he ran the race and included among the supporters who cheered him on to the end were his seventeen grandchildren and his seven great-grandchildren.

Family Race

In 1993 more than one thousand female athletes raced through New York on Sunday, June 20, to compete in the Danskin Tri-athlon Series, an all-women event. The ironic thing about the All-Women Triathlon was that it was held on Father's Day.

Bare Fact

The ancient Greeks gave modern athletes the Olympic Games. The ancient Greeks also believed in having their athletes compete in the buff. In 1991 a group of modern athletes in Florida tried to duplicate ancient Greek athletic tradition by holding the Florida Nude Relays, a serious attempt at running unsanctioned competitive races in the altogether. The Florida Nude Relays took place in May of 1991 after the conclusion of the Florida Relays at Percy Beard Field in Gainesville, Florida. The nude relays were held late at night, understandably so, because sunburn might have been a big problem if the races were held during the day.

Bad Water

American marathon runner Kim Jones had bad luck at a marathon at Sapporo, Japan, in August of 1992. Kim was running with the leaders of the pack when she stopped for water after travelling over nine miles of the course. She dropped her water bottle and when she bent over to pick it up, hurt her back and had to drop out of the race.

Wooden You Like to Try That?

Hendrick Doornekamp, a Dutch distance runner, ran the 1980 New York Marathon while wearing wooden shoes instead of running shoes.

Face Front, Please

Some people thought Ernest Connor didn't know which way was front as they watched him run in the 1980 New York Marathon. Maybe that was because Connor ran all 26 miles and 385 yards of the race backwards.

Sports Animal

Distance runner Samson Kimowba of Kenya sped past England's Chris Stewart during a 15-mile road race in Kenya held in the 1980s. Since the two marathoners had only covered two miles, Stewart couldn't understand why Kimowba was in such a hurry until he looked back over his shoulder. A rhino had crashed out of the undergrowth along the road and was lumbering after them.

Winners Are Losers

Dave Cannon of Great Britain won the Toronto Marathon in 1979. However, after Cannon crossed the finish line to claim his victory he found out he was also a loser. Someone had stolen Dave's warm-up gear, track shoes, and T-shirts, which he'd left behind while he ran the race. The race organizers compensated Dave Cannon for his losses by offering to pay for his stolen items.

Thanks, Pal

American pole vaulter Earl Bell lent one of his vaulting poles to fellow American Dave Roberts at the 1976 U.S. Olympic trials. At the time Bell held the world record in the pole vault at 18 feet 7¼ inches. Roberts repaid Earl Bell's generosity by immediately breaking Bell's record by an inch, using the pole borrowed from his competitor.

Give Him a Hand

Racer Bill Scobey was competing in the Fiesta Bowl Marathon in 1980 when a cheater ran into the pack from the sidelines as the lead runners approached the finish line. Scobey told the phony marathon runner to get off of the course. When the cheater refused to leave the race and dared Scobey to make him leave, 5-foot-7-inch, 125-pound Bill Scobey decided to act. One swift punch sent the dishonest racer tumbling to the pavement, where he sat, stunned, as the legitimate race leaders left him in their dust.

Run-in with the Law

Chris McCabe of Georgetown University paid the price for being a cross-country runner in Washington, D.C., in October of 1980. As McCabe and a group of his cross-country teammates approached a midtown intersection, the traffic light turned yellow and a "don't walk" sign flashed on the face of the runners. The distance runners kept going and were noticed by a policeman who yelled for them to stop. McCabe halted even though his fellow runners didn't. The policeman then issued Chris McCabe a five-dollar summons. The ticket was for "running" a traffic light.

Goofy Golfers

Copy Caddy

Talk about one-upsmanship on the golf links! Larry Harrison and Merdith Henry were playing golf at the Atlantic City Country Club in New Jersey in June of 1980. On the 132-yard 13th hole Larry Harrison hit a wedge shot that took two bounces and dribbled into the cup for a hole in one. Before he could celebrate, Merdith Henry promptly followed Harrison's ace with a wedge shot that bounced only once before skipping into the cup for another hole in one.

That Sinking Feeling

Golf pro Mike Krantz of the United States won the Thailand Open Golf Championship in Bangkok, in 1979, but Mike didn't get a chance to enjoy his victory. Before Krantz could be awarded the King's Cup Trophy which goes to the winner, he collapsed from stomach pains and had to be taken to a hospital. Luckily, Mike recovered to collect his trophy and $6,400 in prize money.

Club Those Guys

Promotors attempted to organize one of the most sexist and distasteful golf tournaments in the history of the sport in Walla Walla, Washington, in 1979. Ron Coleman, a golf pro, tried to coordinate a tournament designed to promote a new line of sport brassieres carried by his pro shop. The tournament, which was for women only, proposed to separate tournament entrants not by their golf handicaps but by their bra sizes. Needless to say, local chapters of NOW, the National Organization for Women, quickly and vehemently protested. The tournament was speedily cancelled and Ron Coleman spent many hours apologizing to everyone offended by the idea.

Talking Sports

Ward Seibert, a school teacher who also works as a caddy, helped Japanese golfer Isao Aoki finish second to American golf legend Jack Nicklaus at the 1980 U.S. Open Tournament. The amazing thing about Seibert's contribution to Aoki's game is that the caddy and golfer didn't speak the same language. Ward Seibert didn't speak any Japanese and Isao Aoki didn't speak any English. Nevertheless the two men were able to communicate during the tournament by using gestures. Obviously some sports have a universal language of their own.

Mommy's Boy

In a way, 25-year-old golfer Oswald Drawdy wasn't able to untie himself from his mother's apron strings even when he qualified to play in the U.S. Open Golf Championships in June of 1993. Drawdy, who qualified for the Open in 1993 after six years of trying, had his mom, Lil Drawdy, caddy for him during the tournament. However, it wasn't a new experience for mother or son. Lil Drawdy had caddied for Oswald about twelve times before, mostly in USGA amateur events.

Oils Well

The Royal and Ancient Golf Club in St. Andrews, Scotland, is a golf course with a history that dates back over 230 years. However, where money is involved, not even golf or its hallowed links are sacred. In 1981, the government granted Premier Consolidated Oilfields a license for exploratory drilling areas that includes the links of the Royal and Ancient Golf Club. There's been no drilling on the links yet and the oil company has no immediate plans for any, but who knows?

Tree Chipper

West German golf pro Bernhard Langer hit a shot that landed up in an ash tree and stuck there during the $180,000 International Open at York, England, in 1981. Rather than take a penalty drop to free his ball from the fork of the tree where it was wedged, Langer decided to play the shot. The West German golfer climbed twenty feet up into the tree and then used a nine iron to whack the wayward ball back onto the course.

One-in-a-Million Shot

Who knows? Maybe that old saying is true. Maybe it *is* better to be lucky than good—even in golf. For 19-year-old Jason Bohn a single stroke of luck on the golf course earned him a lot of money in 1992. Bohn, a college student, was one of twelve finalists in a golf promotion staged to raise money to restore a historic mansion in Alabama. Each golfer had one chance to ace the 135-yard 2nd hole of the University of Alabama's golf course. When Jason recorded the only hole in one, he won the promotion's first prize—one million dollars!

Water on the Brain

Every golfer knows lakes can be a real hazard during an important golf match. Pro golfer Nick Faldo ended up with water on the brain after playing in the second round of the 1993 Masters Tournament. Faldo sank balls in the water on the 11th, 12th, and 13th holes in that round.

No Time Out

Mike Hill was the defending champion of the Senior PGA Bank of Boston Classic Tournament which he was scheduled to play in again in August of 1993. Unfortunately, Hill found out that even reigning champs have to study schedules carefully and always be punctual. Mike Hill didn't check on his starting time for the tournament and when he showed up too late to tee off he was regrettably disqualified by tournament officials and never got the chance to defend his title.

Table Tennis Elbow?

Veteran golf pro Mike Reid missed playing in several PGA tournaments in 1993 due to an injured wrist, which he hurt while playing table tennis. Maybe he "pinged" when he should have "ponged."

A Big Hit with Nicklaus

Famous pro golfer Jack Nicklaus shot a birdie at the 1983 Colonial National Invitation Golf Tournament, with a little help from a golf fan. On the 14th hole of the tourney's course in Fort Worth, Texas, Nicklaus hit an approach shot that flew past the green and hit a fan, Belinda Williams. The ball bounced off Ms. Williams and onto the green, stopping about three feet from the cup. Jack Nicklaus then tapped it in to record his fan-aided birdie!

Snakes Alive!

The 1975 Malaysian Open Golf Tournament was full of hidden hazards for pro golfer Howard Twitty. In the middle of the round Twitty's caddy, a native of Malaysia, dropped Howard's bag and began yelling as he ran away from it. Howard Twitty watched in shock and amazement as a King Cobra snake slithered out of the bag. How it got in there no one ever found out.

Missing from the Links

Golf pro Raymond Floyd felt that he had no chance of making the cut of the Tournament Players Championship in 1982 after he shot two mediocre rounds, so he packed his bags at Ponto Vedra Beach, Florida, and went home to Miami. Floyd never figured that with 63 golfers still left to finish the second round when he left, the cut total would be 148, which is what Floyd, the defending champion, had shot.

Imagine Ray Floyd's amazement the next day, as he was pulling weeds in his garden, when his wife rushed out of their house to inform him he was still eligible to play in the tournament. Floyd received the shocking good news at 11:30 in the morning. His scheduled tee time back at the tournament was 12:36! Ray Floyd grabbed his gear, chartered a jet, reserved a helicopter, and jumped into his car. He sped to a private airport and hopped on a Lear jet. The jet took off and landed at a field fifteen miles from the course. Floyd raced to a waiting helicopter which transported him to the tournament site. He then jumped on a golf cart and zoomed to his tee, arriving there with just thirty seconds to spare. Hastily he took two practice swings and teed off. Ray ended up finishing 23rd in the tourney, but just managing to get there proved to be quite a success story!

Electrifying Player

Lee Trevino's great skill with a golf club electrified many fans over the years. However, at the 1975 Western Open Golf Tournament, Lee had a truly electrifying experience. He was hit by a lightning bolt on the 13th hole on the 13th day of the month. Luckily, Lee recovered to win many tournaments after that awful experience, but he considers the number thirteen to be bad luck for him—with good reason.

Foxy Hazard

The Longview Golf Course in Timonium, Maryland, had a strange hazard in the 1980s. A red fox lived in the woods near the 11th hole and would often dart out onto the course when golf balls landed near its home turf. The fox would snatch up a ball in its mouth and then scoot back into the woods with it. Officials at the club estimated that the foxy hazard of the Maryland course claimed over 350 golf balls!

Splashdown

When Jerry Pate took first place at the Danny Thomas–Memphis Classic Golf Tournament in 1981 it was his first major victory in almost three years. Pate celebrated his triumph by diving headfirst into the lake on the 18th green. His victory celebration made quite a splash with everyone who witnessed it.

Not a Birdie

In June of 1993 golfer Larry Bieker hit a tee shot at Haynes Center Golf Club in Nebraska that hit a bird flying by. The ball then dropped out of the sky and into the cup on the par-3 6th hole for a hole in one!

Big, Big Hazard

The Hans Merensky Country Club had a big hazard on the 17th hole of its golf course in the late 1980s. The Hans Merensky Country Club is in Phalaborwa, South Africa, and several families of hippos lived in the pools that formed the water hazard on the club's 17th hole.

Don't Bee Upset

Sally Little won the $100,000 LPGA Tournament in 1979 despite the fact that she was stung in the throat by a bee after her tee shot on the 17th hole. Ice was applied to Little's neck and she continued on, playing well enough to ice her victory over defending champion Pat Bradley.

Broken Record

Jerry Smagala's swing felt funny when he teed off with a 5-iron on the par-3, 179-yard 5th hole at Falls Road Golf Course in Potomac, Maryland, in 1979. Smagala, of Annandale, Virginia, checked out his club and noticed that the club's head had broken off when he'd hit the ball. Nevertheless the ball that he'd hit landed in the cup for a hole in one.

Don't Bug Me

Golfer Judy Rankin missed a seemingly easy 10-foot putt at the $150,000 LPGA Tournament at Dearborn, Michigan, in 1979 which caused her to finish in second place. When Judy explained why she missed the putt she put the blame on being bugged. Rankin said a fly landed on her ball just as she putted and the insect disturbed her concentration.

Grid Irony

Fine with Me

Tackle David Williams of the Houston Oilers had a difficult choice to make during the 1993 NFL season. Williams' choice was between football and fatherhood. When David Williams' wife, Debi, gave birth to the couple's first child, Scot, a 9-pound, 15-ounce boy on Saturday, October 16, 1993, David decided to stay with his wife and child in a hospital in Houston and skip playing in the Oilers' game on Sunday, October 17, 1993, against the Patriots in New England.

The Oilers had given David permission to miss practices and meetings during the week to be with his wife, but expected their starting tackle to attend the game against New England. When Williams chose fatherhood over football, he was fined a week's pay by the Houston organization which amounted to over $100,000. David Williams considered the fatherhood-fine money well spent and returned to playing football for the Houston Oilers the following week. In a way, David's son, Scot, was a football bonus baby in the truest sense of the word.

Foreign Footballer

A lot of American football fans don't realize that their beloved sport is played on many foreign shores. The city of Bolzano in Italy is actually the home of two semi-professional football teams. The Bolzano Jets play in Italy's A-1 League (the most competitive league) while the Bolzano New Giants play in the A-2 League (slightly less competitive). Both teams utilize a few American ex-college athletes, who are paid players. The remainder of the teams' rosters are filled out with non-paid, part-time Italian athletes who have regular daytime jobs.

In 1992 James Grant, an American player who starred at Ramapo College in New Jersey, was the starting quarterback for the New Giants. Unfortunately for Grant he didn't speak a word of

Italian and all but one of his offensive teammates could not understand English. How could a quarterback call plays in the huddle when there was a difficult language barrier? Actually, it didn't turn out to be much of a problem at all. Bolzano's offensive coordinator, Enrico Tecchiati, who understood English and also played offensive guard for the New Giants, translated Grant's words into Italian in the huddle and everyone got the right message about which play was called.

Flushed with Rage

The Penn State vs. Ohio State game of 1978 matched up two great college coaches. Penn State was coached by Joe Paterno and Ohio State was coached by Woody Hayes. Prior to the big matchup Penn State Nittany Lion fans showed what they thought of their rival squad's mentor in a funny way. They distributed toilet paper bearing the likeness of Woody Hayes on every paper square.

Halloween Scare

Nose tackle Dan Saleaumua of the Kansas City Chiefs had quite a scare during the Chiefs' game against the Miami Dolphins on Halloween Day, 1993. Saleaumua was on the sidelines standing near the official who fired a blank gun to signal the end of the game's first half. The official didn't notice the big tackle behind him and fired the gun so close to Dan Saleaumua's head that residue from the blank shot hit him in the eyes. Luckily, Saleaumua was wearing contacts and wasn't seriously injured; but the noise scared him half to death.

Wrong Combination

Eddie Walker, a wide receiver for the Rutgers University Scarlet Knights, missed about a week of football practice during the 1993 season because of a crazy injury. Walker twisted his back while trying to get something out of his locker in the locker room.

Band Aided

When the Texas A&M Aggies squared off against the University of Texas Longhorns on the gridiron on November 26, 1992, the two teams didn't show each other much respect. The Aggies upstaged Texas even before the game began when A&M's football players ran through the Texas band as it marched off the field after putting on a pregame show. When the first half ended, the Texas Longhorn footballers returned the disrespect by racing through the A&M band as it marched off the field after putting on its halftime show. However, the most disrespectful demonstration of all occurred after the Aggies defeated the Longhorns 34 to 13. Players from the A&M team ran out to mid-field after the game ended and performed a taunting dance aimed at the Longhorns' sideline. It was the ultimate show of no respect.

Losing Is Hard to Swallow

Football coach Grant Teaff of Baylor swallowed a five-inch earthworm prior to Baylor's game against heavily favored Texas in 1978 in an attempt to psych up his team. Apparently the coach's recipe for success worked, as Baylor devoured Texas on the gridiron that day by the score of 38–14.

Snow Dough

Blizzard conditions didn't stop the 1985 NFL game between the Tampa Bay Buccaneers and the Green Bay Packers played at the Packers' home site, Lambeau Field. However, the heavy snow did cause several unusual delays. In fact, the opening kickoff of the gridiron contest had to be delayed 20 seconds as officials searched for the coin used in the pregame flip which had fallen to the ground and gotten lost in a small snowdrift.

Musical Note

Football coach Woody Hayes, who led Ohio State to many great winning seasons, was very serious about competition in the Big Ten. He once berated the Ohio State Marching Band because he felt his school's band was outplayed by the Michigan band during a game.

Shocking Speech

In 1969 Clive Rush, the new head coach of the New England (formerly Boston) Patriots, was introduced to the media at a press conference. After Rush was presented to the group of reporters gathered for the occasion by team officials, Clive picked up a microphone to make a few choice opening remarks. To the amazement of the crowd, instead of delivering the usual gridiron pep talk, Clive Rush clutched the mike tightly in his hand and began to screech in agony. The cause of Rush's sudden torture was a faulty microphone wire that sent jolts of powerful electric shocks pulsating through the body of the helpless head coach. Rush twitched in pain and screamed at the top of his lungs until someone finally had the good sense to pull the mike's plug out of the wall socket. Luckily Rush wasn't seriously injured. However, that freak accident proved to be a painfully shocking introduction to the New England press for Clive Rush.

Name Shame

Quarterback Gino Torretta of the University of Miami won the Heisman Trophy as college football's best player in 1992, but wasn't always shown the respect he deserved for his many gridiron accomplishments. That same year Torretta won the Johnny Unitas Award as America's Best College Quarterback, but when he received his plaque he was shocked to discover that his name was spelled incorrectly on the award.

Painfully Funny

Talk about a freak injury! Quarterback Scott Semptimphelter of Lehigh University suffered an odd injury in 1993. During Lehigh's victory over Pennsylvania rival Lafayette College in the final gridiron contest of the year for both schools, Semptimphelter missed the final fourteen minutes of the gridiron matchup because he suffered a ruptured Achilles tendon. Did the Lehigh quarterback injure himself while tossing one of the four touchdown passes he completed in that game? Nope! He hurt himself jumping up and down on the field's sidelines in celebration of an interception made by a Lehigh defensive player.

No Goals for Winning

Winning isn't everything. Football fans at Northwestern proved that on November 7, 1981, when Northwestern lost to Michigan State by the score of 61 to 14 to set a record for football futility. The loss was Northwestern's 29th in a row, which at the time established an NCAA record. To celebrate the infamous feat, Northwestern fans tore down their team's goalpost.

Like Father, Like Son

Bum Phillips was dismissed as the head coach of the New Orleans Saints late in the 1985 NFL season. However, Bum probably didn't feel too badly about getting axed because he thought very highly of his successor. The coach who was appointed to take Phillips' job was Wade Phillips, Bum's son!

Hands Down, Please

In 1986 Louisiana State University's field-goal kicker Ronnie Lewis was jeered by the crowd during the Tigers' unexpected loss to Miami of Ohio at Baton Rouge, Louisiana. Losing his cool, Lewis responded with an obscene hand gesture using both hands. When a photo of Ronnie's angry two-finger salute to the fans appeared in a Baton Rouge newspaper, the Tigers' head coach, Bill Arnsparger, tried to explain his player's temperamental display. Arnsparger said Ronnie Lewis was just signalling to the stands that his team was number 11.

Dream Team

In 1980 offensive tackle Vernon Holland of the Cincinnati Bengals told reporters he'd dreamed that he had been traded. When a reporter asked Holland which team he had been traded to in his dreams, Vernon replied, "I don't know who got me. I dream in black-and-white so I couldn't tell what color the uniforms were."

Dragging Your Wagon

To celebrate Oklahoma scoring against rival Colorado in the two teams' 1993 meeting, Oklahoma's mascot, the horse-drawn Sooner Schooner (a covered wagon), made a victory trip out onto the field. As it did, the Sooner Schooner turned over and crashed on its side.

Delay Hooray!

Bernards High School in Bernardsville, New Jersey, suffered through some tough times on the gridiron in the late 1980s and early 1990s. The Mountaineers of Bernards High played 41 high-school football games from 1987 to 1992 without winning a single one. To make matters worse, several unusual things occurred during that embarrassing losing streak. For example, when Bernards lost to Glen Ridge High School for its 33rd consecutive loss in 1991, the score was appropriately 33–0 in favor of Glen Ridge.

In 1992 the losing streak continued but the Mountaineers had high hopes of ending their 41-game skid without a victory when they met Bayley-Ellard High on October 4, 1992. The Mountaineers showed up at Bayley-Ellard's field eager to play and hopeful of a win at last. The squad went through its pregame drills with great zeal and then prepared for the opening kickoff by exhibiting immense confidence and enthusiasm. However, a slight stumbling block appeared which prevented the Mountaineers from ending their losing streak on October 4. The team and coaches showed up for the game and ready to play, but no officials showed up for the game and the contest had to be postponed until the following day. Undaunted by the ill-fated turn of events, the Bernards High Mountaineers showed up for the contest against Bayley-Ellard the following day, and ended the team's 41-game losing streak by winning the game 22 to 19 on a last-second score.

Don't Nod Your Head

Linebacker John Roper of the Dallas Cowboys got more rest than he wanted when he nodded off during a team meeting in 1993. After head coach Jimmy Johnson caught Roper snoozing, John was dropped from the Cowboys' squad.

Loony Logic

Montana State football coach Ray Jenkins didn't let the fact that his team hadn't won a single game in 1958 upset him when he was asked about the prospects of his 1959 squad. Coach Jenkins quipped, "We definitely will be improved this year. Last year we lost ten games. This year we only scheduled nine."

Ground Game

Troubles persisted for the New Orleans Saints even after the Pittsburgh Steelers whipped them 37–14 in an NFL game in October of 1993. When the Saints team travelled to the airport for their flight home to New Orleans, the trip was delayed because a small motor on the left wing of the team plane suddenly exploded and caught fire. After a 2½-hour delay, the motor was repaired and the Saints finally winged their way home.

Holy Cats!

What do the Columbia Lions and the Northwestern Wildcats have in common, other than nicknames that relate to cats? The answer is that both of those schools had less than purr-fect outings on the football gridiron during the 1970s and 1980s. Northwestern set a record by losing 34 straight football games from 1979 to 1982 before finally snapping its dismal streak with a win over Northern Illinois. Then along came Columbia with its cat's eye on the record. From 1983 to 1988 Columbia lost 44 games in a row to set a new low mark for losing streaks in college football before finally besting Princeton in 1988. *Me-yeow!* Now those are surely two tales of woe.

Crank Call

Somehow, someone changed the phone recording normally used at the Minnesota Vikings' offices in 1991. Instead of the regular recorded message, callers to that NFL team heard this angry crank response instead: "Thank you for calling the most rotten, stinking team in the history of man. That's right, you have reached the Minnesota Vikings." Of course, the nasty response was quickly erased soon after the substituted message was discovered.

Snow Job

San Francisco 49er field-goal kicker Ray Wersching trotted onto the field in Colorado on November 13, 1985, to attempt an important field goal against the Denver Broncos. The 49ers were trailing the Broncos 14–3 on a snowy day in Denver and Wersching's 19-yard chip shot would cut the Broncos' lead if the short kick was good. San Francisco lined up for the field goal confident that Wersching would easily split the uprights. However, just as the ball was snapped, a snowball came flying out of the end-zone stands. The snowball landed on the field between the center, who snapped the football, and the holder, whose job it was to catch the ball and place it down for Wersching's attempt. The snowball shattered into hundreds of pieces and it also shattered the holder's concentration. Distracted by the snowball exploding in front of him, San Francisco holder Matt Cavanaugh bobbled the football and Ray Wersching never got a chance to attempt the aborted field goal. The 49ers ended up losing the game 17–16 and the Broncos iced the win with a little help from a well-aimed snowball thrown by an unidentified fan.

Kidnapping Kidder

Defensive tackle Alfred Oglesby made headlines when he briefly disappeared in July of 1992 and was late returning to the Miami Dolphins training camp at St. Thomas University in Miami's Dade County. When Oglesby finally appeared at camp and explained his reason for being tardy to head coach Don Shula, Shula could barely believe his ears. Alfred Oglesby claimed that he had been kidnapped by two armed gunmen who wanted to steal the borrowed BMW car Alfred was driving. Oglesby further stated that he had been dumped out in the Florida Everglades by the kidnappers—who then rode off in the car, leaving Alfred to find his way back to civilization on foot.

Alfred's kidnapping tale seemed almost too frightening to be true. In fact, it wasn't true at all. After an investigation by police officials, Oglesby regretfully confessed that the entire kidnapping story was pure fiction. The big tackle had made it all up to escape the wrath of Coach Don Shula for reporting late back to camp. In truth Alfred Oglesby had overslept at a rented house where he had been staying with another Miami veteran. Coach Shula fined his big tackle and warned him to curb his overactive imagination in the future.

Tape Player

Days after tackle Alfred Oglesby came up with a wild whopper as an excuse for being late to a practice at the Miami Dolphins' training camp in July of 1992, he was punished for telling lies by his teammates. Alfred, who originally claimed he was abducted at gunpoint which delayed his arrival at practice instead of confessing that he'd just overslept, really *was* abducted—by Miami Dolphin players who snatched the 280-pound tackle out of his room at St. Thomas University in Florida. The players then duct-taped Alfred Oglesby to a tree outside the team's sleeping quarters. Oglesby screamed and kicked for about twenty-five minutes before his vigilante teammates finally set him free. Someone should have reminded Alfred that the truth will always set one free.

Running Game

Union High School football coach Lou Rettino made it a policy to always take time to talk to the press after a game. Rettino's willingness to satisfy reporters almost proved costly to the New Jersey high school coach in 1993. After Union defeated Kearny High School 42–6 in September of that year, Rettino was answering reporters' questions in the parking lot of the Kearny school when he saw the Union team bus pull out and head for home. Coach Rettino had to race after the bus and flag it down to save himself from a long walk home.

Bad Nudes Bares

The National Football League had its own unique version of a cover-up in 1978. After a member of the San Diego Chargers' cheering squad (called the Chargettes) posed unclothed for some photographs, the NFL owners took a stand on cheerleaders who entertained any thoughts of baring it all. Pete Rozelle, the NFL Commissioner at the time, issued a league ruling that forbade cheerleaders for National Football League teams from posing for any photographs while completely out of uniform.

Welcome Back

Johnny Rodgers, who won the Heisman Trophy in 1972 while playing football for Nebraska, didn't get much of a chance to admire the trophy he received for being college football's top player. Attorney Henry Ramirez held the Heisman Trophy from 1987 to 1993 as collateral against money he claimed was owed to him by Johnny Rodgers. When Ramirez finally agreed to return the trophy to Rodgers in September of 1993, Johnny felt like a winner again.

Double Coaching

Glenn "Pop" Warner was one of the greatest college football coaches in the long history of the gridiron game. Warner coached the immortal Jim Thorpe at Carlisle and also coached players at Pittsburgh, Iowa State, Georgia, and Cornell. The funny fact of

Warner's outstanding coaching career is that on several occasions he coached two college teams at the same time.

In 1895 and 1896 Pop Warner was the coach of Iowa State and the coach of Georgia simultaneously. In 1897 and 1898 Pop coached Iowa State and Cornell simultaneously. Finally in 1899 Glenn "Pop" Warner coached Iowa State and Carlisle both at the same time. How did it happen? In those days dual coaching was permitted, so Pop Warner coached Iowa State early one season and then acted as Iowa State's advisor while turning over the actual coaching reins to assistants. Pop was then free to spend the rest of the seasons coaching other schools. So from 1895 to 1899 Pop Warner was officially the coach of two different colleges simultaneously. Coaching two teams was a good way for Warner to make enough money to live on, as coaches were greatly underpaid in those days. Luckily for everyone involved, none of the teams Pop Warner coached at the same time ever played each other during those years.

A Lot of Hot Air

Auburn's Terry Daniel was one of America's top punters in 1993. In fact, his punting average was so astounding that season that opposing coach Jackie Sherrill of rival Mississippi State wondered if the ball Daniel booted in the game against him actually contained ordinary, run-of-the-mill air.

In Auburn's game against Mississippi State on October 9, 1993, Terry Daniel punted for a 56.5-yard average. Officials from Mississippi State suspected that the football Daniel booted might actually contain helium instead of ordinary air and requested an investigation. The footballs used in the contest were confiscated and tested. They proved to be filled with ordinary air. Later testing also showed that balls filled with helium travelled no further, and even a little less, than footballs filled with regular air. The entire incident proved to be a lot of hot air about nothing.

Hold Up!

Runningback Larry Smith of Florida scored a touchdown in the 1967 Orange Bowl which helped his team beat Georgia Tech.

Smith scampered 94 yards for a score in that contest, but had trouble with his pants. At the Georgia Tech 35-yard line, Larry's pants started to fall down and he had to use one hand to hold them up as he continued on his way into the end zone. Luckily Larry's end zone remained covered up.

Name Game

Cleveland Browns wide receiver Michael Jackson began the 1993 NFL year by wearing number one on his jersey. When NFL officials warned that Jackson couldn't wear number one because receivers must wear numbers in the eighties, Jackson agreed to change his number to eighty-one before the team's first game. However, Jackson also decided to change his name. Michael's mom's last name was Jackson but his father's last name was Dyson. So to honor his dad, Michael Jackson became Michael Dyson for Cleveland's first game of the regular season. But the story didn't end there. Youngsters who were fans of the Cleveland wide receiver pleaded with him to go back to using the name they knew him by, which was Jackson. Michael Jackson agreed, and returned to being Michael Jackson for the remainder of the season.

Don't Rush Out

In college Bernie Kosar and Vinny Testaverde were great passing quarterbacks while playing for the University of Miami. However, Kosar and Testaverde were not the greatest at running the ball. Bernie Kosar completed his college career with a net rushing average of −386 yards while Vinny Testaverde finished his college career with a net rushing average of −320 yards. Apparently those quarterback sacks really do add up.

Cheerful Mom

Talk about team spirit! When Vicki Peake heard that the Houston Oilers were holding tryouts for their cheerleading squad in April of 1992, she was determined not to let anything stand in the way of her chance to cheer for the NFL team. Peake, who had cheered previously for the Chicago Blitz of the United States Football League, appeared at the April 28 tryout even though she was pregnant and due to give birth in a matter of days. The judges at the tryout truly admired Vicky's enthusiasm and spirit, but advised her to get her doctor's permission before doing any Oiler cheers and invited her back to try out at a later date.

Food for Thought

Quarterback Tommy Kramer of the Minnesota Vikings bought seventy dollars' worth of hamburgers as a culinary reward for his offensive linemen after they kept the defense from sacking him even once in a 1985 game. After the offensive line produced a second sack-free game for Kramer a short time later, Viking center Jim Howell demanded a richer prize. He told his quarterback he and his fellow offensive linemen had had their fill of burgers and now expected a reward of prime rib!

Long-Distance Celebration

Boston College football fans were jubilant when the underdog Boston College Eagles travelled to Notre Dame in November of 1993 and managed to upset the Fightin' Irish team, which was undefeated and ranked number one in the country at the time. The Eagles' fans at Boston College were so thrilled over their team's 41–39 win over the Irish on the road that they rushed into Boston College's home field (Alumni Stadium) and tore down the goalposts, even though the game had actually been played elsewhere.

Fear Factor

In November of 1956 St. Louis Cardinals quarterback Lamar McHan was named his team's starting QB for a game against the Pittsburgh Steelers. Instead of being eager to play, McHan asked his head coach to remove his name from the lineup because he was just too nervous to start the game. Lamar McHan's wish was granted and he was also fined three thousand dollars, which didn't do much to soothe his frayed nerves.

A Kick Out of Comedy

King-Size Headaches

King Edward III of England viewed the game of soccer as an idle practice and tried to do away with it. Edward III felt that soccer kept his subjects from practising archery, which was not only a sport but a skill necessary for protection. Even though Edward III tried to ban soccer in the mid-1300s, the English kept playing the game anyway. Subsequent English kings were also against the game. Richard I, Henry IV, and Henry VIII all tried to discourage their subjects from playing soccer but failed. Soccer was as popular in England back then as it is today.

Grounded

English soccer player Steve Morrow scored the winning goal for his Arsenal team at London's Wembley Stadium in April of 1993. His teammates were so happy they rushed out and lifted Steve onto their shoulders and then tossed him up into the air. Unfortunately, however, they forgot to catch him and Steve crashed to the ground, breaking his arm when he landed.

Double Header

Andranik Eskandarian and Ivan Buljan of the New York Cosmos of the North American Soccer League had a run-in with each other while warming up for the Cosmos' game against the Toronto Sting team in 1981. Eskandarian and Buljan were testing the astroturf surface of Toronto's Exhibition Stadium during a warm-up work-out when they crashed into each other headfirst. Andranik Eskandarian was shaken up but not seriously injured. His teammate, Ivan Buljan, ended up getting a black eye and several stitches to close a gash in his scalp. Sometimes even professionals need to remember that players should always keep their heads up or at least watch where they're going.

Forget This

A heated college-soccer contest between Trenton State College and West Chester College, which was played in New Jersey in October of 1992, ended in a very strange way. After a Trenton State player was upended in the penalty area by the West Chester goalie, referee Alex Ivahnenko awarded Trenton State a penalty kick and kicked the West Chester goalie out of the game. Since the rules call for a player on the field to face a penalty kick, the referee wouldn't allow West Chester coach Kendall Walkes to replace the team's ejected goalie with the squad's backup goalie, who was on the bench. Coach Walkes angrily refused to allow any of his players on the field at the time of the infraction to face the Trenton State player for the penalty kick. A heated discussion over the call lasted for about thirty minutes. Finally referee Alex Ivahnenko called the game a one-to-one tie and declared it over, even though there was still 20:13 to play in the contest.

Chill Out, Dude

A game between Sacramento and Las Vegas in the American Soccer League in August of 1979 ended in a bizarre fashion when a player for Las Vegas flipped out over getting kicked in the leg. Miodrag Lacevic, a forward for Las Vegas, was kicked by a Sacramento player in a leg which Lacevic had broken earlier in the season. Angrily Lacevic then kicked the Sacramento player back. That ignited a scuffle between other players on both teams. When referee Peter Verezcky tried to eject Miodrag Lacevic for his part in starting the trouble, Lacevic lost his temper and chased the referee around the stadium. Finally Lacevic cooled down and started to leave the field when he spotted the Sacramento player who had kicked him. Miodrag then picked up a handful of sand and threw it at the player. The sand touched off another skirmish between the teams' players. When some of the irate Sacramento players chased Miodrag Lacevic into the stands, the mad Las Vegas forward got into another scuffle, this time with a spectator, and had to be removed by stadium security guards. For losing his cool in such a wild way, Miodrag Lacevic also lost his place on the Las Vegas team and was later dropped from the squad by his coach.

The Shirt Off His Back

Fidel Castro, the dictator of Cuba and a big soccer fan, sent Argentine striker Diego Maradona a message of congratulations when Maradona scored his first goal back with an Argentine club after spending years of playing for teams in Spain and Italy. To repay Castro for his note Maradona sent the Cuban dictator a thank-you message after Diego played in Argentina's 1–0 victory over Australia in November of 1993, which qualified Argentina for World Cup competition. However, Diego Maradona didn't just scribble his note to Castro on paper. He wrote it on the soccer shirt he wore while playing against Australia and sent the entire shirt to Fidel Castro. Maradona literally gave Fidel Castro the shirt off his back.

Shaky Sport

A soccer game between the Ecuadorean National Team and Argentina's Newells Old Boys Team had to be cancelled for a shaky reason in August of 1981. An earthquake had shaken the Ecuadorean team's stadium and engineers were not certain the stadium stands were safe.

A Perfect Ten

Brazil's Pele is one of the most famous soccer stars in the world. During his playing days Pele believed the number 10 was good luck for him and always wore it on his jersey. However, when Pele entered World Cup play in 1958 he found out not even stars get to pick the number they want to wear on their jerseys. Pele and other star players on his team had to draw for a number to wear for the World Cup, which was held in Sweden that year. Since there are sixteen to eighteen players on a World Cup team, Pele's odds of getting the number he wanted were not very promising. Nevertheless, when Pele randomly drew his number for the 1958 World Cup he amazingly selected number 10 by pure chance. If you think that was lucky, consider what happened at the 1962 World Cup held in Chile. Again Pele had to randomly pick a number to wear, and again he picked his lucky number, 10. As far as Pele was concerned, luck had made the Brazilian soccer star a perfect ten for life.

Bee Careful

A fireworks display at a 1982 soccer match in the Brazilian city of Presidente Prudente angered a huge swarm of bees nesting nearby. The angry bees attacked spectators at the match and about two hundred soccer fans were stung by the furious insects.

Unexpected Guests

When the Dynamo Kiev Boys Soccer Team arrived in Florida from the Ukraine to play in the 1992 International Firecracker Tournament, the sponsors of the tourney were caught a bit off guard. A member of the Kiev team (which was made up of young boys) phoned a tournament official a little after midnight on the Friday before the weekend tourney to announce he and his teammates were waiting at the Miami Airport to be picked up. The official at the other end of the line was a bit shocked. The sponsors of the International Firecracker Tournament had thought the Dynamo Kiev team had cancelled its scheduled trip and they weren't expecting the boys. Nevertheless everything worked out. The unexpected boys team was picked up at the airport by tournament officials and arrangements were hastily made to accommodate them for their stay in America. The Kiev team generously repaid their hosts by winning the International Firecracker Tournament and outscoring their opponents by a total of 27 goals to none!

A Hot Soccer Match

Some mindless soccer fans of a West German soccer club accidentally set several train cars on fire in 1981 as their train sped from West Berlin to Aachen, a city on the German–Belgian border. The fans on the train were travelling to Aachen to see their team play a soccer match. The fire started when rockets and other fireworks were ignited by soccer fans in one of the cars. Damage was estimated at nearly $2,000,000. The train had to make an emergency stop before its destination and most of the three hundred soccer fans on board had to return home to Berlin without seeing their team play.

Net Loss

The City University of New York soccer team wasn't exactly a powerhouse on the field during the late 1970s. The CUNY soccer squad went almost five years without winning a single soccer match. The team played 65 games starting in 1975 and ending in 1980 without any victories (64 losses, 1 tie). Finally, in October of 1980, CUNY ended its long losing streak with a 1–0 forfeit win over Hunter College. The forfeit was due to the fact that the Hunter team never showed up to play the game.

Mooned

A Buffalo, New York, high school soccer coach quit his job at Amherst Central High School in 1980 because of a problem with moons. After two of his players mooned passersby by exposing their buttocks from the team bus on the ride home from a game in nearby Rochester, the coach disciplined the players by withholding various campus privileges and their varsity letters. When school authorities refused to uphold his punishment, the soccer mentor called it quits. Scientists do agree that the moon has strange effects on some people.

Hot Tempered

After the Dutch soccer team of FC Den Haag lost to rival Haarlem by the score of 4–1 in April of 1982, Den Haag fans were so enraged they rioted and set fire to their team's home stadium. Before the blaze was extinguished, the flames caused $500,000 worth of damages.

Knocked Silly

Nose Dive

Evander Holyfield squared off against Riddick Bowe at the Caesars Palace Outdoor Stadium on the evening of November 6, 1993. At stake in their bout was the World Boxing Association Heavyweight title. As the two boxers met in the middle of the ring round after round, an unexpected guest circled high above the stadium waiting for a chance to drop in at the championship event. The eyes of the 15,000 fight fans on hand that night were fixed on the fighters, so paraglider James Miller, a thirty-year-old boxing fan and sky diver went unnoticed as he winged his way out of the dark clouds towards the lighted ring below. When parachutist Miller landed unexpectedly against the ring ropes midway through the seventh round, spectators, television crewpeople, and especially the boxers were shocked and stunned by his sudden appearance. The fighters, who were in a clinch at the time of the parachutist's arrival, were quickly separated by the referee and the fight was halted for what proved to be a 21-minute delay. The fans at ringside were so angered by the skydiver's uninvited appearance that they began to attack and punch him. Miller had to be rescued by security guards, who then hustled him off to jail where he was processed and released after posting bail. Evander Holyfield meanwhile went on to reclaim his title from champion Riddick Bowe despite the rude interruption provided by the uninvited parachutist.

Knocked Down but Not Out

Boxer Barry Roberts knocked down opponent Jack Russell during their fight for the Australian Junior Flyweight title which was held in Sydney, Australia, in January of 1993. Roberts decked Russell in the ninth round but then hit his dazed foe again while he was still down and was therefore disqualified by the referee. It was one of those odd moments in boxing when a fighter lost a bout while knocking down his opponent.

Big Loss

While boxer John Tate was in the ring losing his WBA Heavyweight Crown to Mike Weaver in April of 1980, Tate and his manager, Ace Miller, were also losing other things. During the fight, which was held in the basketball arena of Tennessee University, thieves broke into the deserted home of champion John Tate. The crooks made off with jewelry and rifles valued at $100,000 that belonged to both Tate and Miller. Some nights you just can't win at anything!

Pow! Wow!

WBC middleweight champion Gerald McClellan didn't even work up a sweat in defense of his title against Jay Bell in their fight held in Puerto Rico on August 6, 1993. At the sound of the opening bell McClellan rushed out and landed a powerful left hook to Bell's kidneys which swiftly sent the challenger to the canvas. Jay Bell was quickly counted out just twenty seconds into the fight. Gerald McClellan's twenty-second kayo was the fastest knockout in title-fight history.

Big Bluffer

Ed Dunkhorst weighed in at 312 pounds for his heavyweight fight against an opponent who tipped the scales at a mere 172 pounds. Most people on hand for that heavyweight bout in April of 1990 figured the fight would be no contest. It wasn't! Heavyweight champ Bob Fitzsimmons, who weighed just 172 pounds, kayoed 312-pound Ed Dunkhorst in the second round of their ring battle.

Fair Exchange

Light welterweight boxers Gert Bo Jacobsen of Denmark and Chris McCallum of Scotland exchanged a fair amount of punches during the opening of their fight in Copenhagen in October of 1982. In fact Jacobsen and McCallum knocked each other down simultaneously when they traded punches in the first round. Both fighters hit the canvas at the same time, but Jacobsen got quickly to his feet while McCallum received an eight count. When Chris McCallum finally did get up, Gert Bo Jacobsen sent him back to the canvas for good with a powerful right cross that won the bout for the Danish fighter.

Tough Talk

WBC super welterweight champion Terry Norris repeatedly boasted loudly to the media that he was the greatest fighter pound-for-pound in the world, before his bout with Simon Brown in December of 1993. Unfortunately, talk proved to be cheap when the fighters met in the ring. Brown, the challenger, who had little to say prior to the fight, knocked out Norris in the fourth round of their title fight.

Punch the Time Clock

When Lloyd Honeyghan met Gene Hatcher for the WBC welterweight championship at Marbella, Spain, in August of 1987, the title was decided rather quickly. Honeyghan won the welterweight crown by knocking out Hatcher forty seconds after the fight started.

Price Fight

Heavyweight champ Mike Tyson met challenger Michael Spinks in a title fight held at Atlantic City in June of 1988. Tyson retained his title and made short work of Spinks. The challenger, Michael Spinks, was knocked out one minute and thirty-one seconds after the opening bell. For his work in that brief battle, Mike Tyson was well paid. In fact, he earned $219,780 per second for his one minute and thirty-one seconds of work. Or, if you want to put it in boxing terms, for the eight punches Tyson landed on Spinks, the champion earned 2.5 million per punch for a total of some $20,000,000.

Beer Facts

When Marvin Hagler of the United States won the undisputed middleweight boxing crown by beating Britain's Alan Minter in September of 1980, English fight fans on hand for the bout in Wembley, England, didn't just grin and bear their disappointment. After Hagler stopped Minter in the third round, fans of the fallen English fighter, upset by the referee's decision to halt the bout, started flinging beer cans and bottles into the ring. The barrage continued for several minutes. Later, some fans who were identified as can throwers were arrested and sentenced to two months in jail.

Toast of the Ring

The odds were against Belgian boxer Jean Pierre Coopman beating reigning heavyweight champion Muhammad Ali in their title fight in February of 1976, and no one knew it better than Coopman. Nevertheless, the underdog challenger, who was known as "the lion of Flanders," decided to enjoy his ring encounter with one of the best boxers in history.

Every time Jean Pierre returned to his corner after a round ended during the fight, he took a swig from a mysterious-looking quart-size bottle covered with thick white tape. While Ali enjoyed the fight by landing punches at will, Coopman seemed to enjoy drinking from the bottle between rounds. After Muhammad Ali put a merciful stop to the uneven bout by kayoing Coopman in the 5th round, the contents of Jean Pierre's mystery bottle was finally discovered. Jean Pierre Coopman had been sipping champagne all through the fight!

Hands Off

Gregorio Benitez worked as a cornerman for his son, champion welterweight boxer Wilfredo Benitez, during Wilfredo's title defense against Harold Weston in 1979. Gregorio was so angered by his son's performance during that fight that he lost his cool. An infuriated Gregorio Benitez smacked his son with his hand as Wilfredo sat on his stool after the twelfth round ended. At the start of the thirteenth round Wilfredo Benitez came out punching and won a close decision over Harold Weston.

All Fired Up

When the WBA Junior Featherweight championship fight between Thai challenger Vichitmuangroi-et and champion Ricardo Cardona of Colombia at Roi Et, Thailand, was unexpectedly cancelled in March of 1979, Thai boxing fans were so upset that they set fire to the boxing ring.

Tennis Court Jesters

Skirting the Issue

Martina Navratilova had an easy time defeating Andrea Jaeger in the 1983 Women's Finals at Wimbledon. Martina's game held up well as she cruised to victory over Jaeger, but unfortunately Navratilova's skirt didn't hold up quite as well during the match. The problem began during a key rally. Ms. Navratilova's skirt began to slip off as she returned shot after shot. Undaunted by a falling skirt, Martina continued to play, holding her racket in one hand and holding up her skirt with her other hand. When there was a break in the action, Ms. Navratilova used a safety pin to solve the problem of a loosely fitting skirt and then went on to capture the Wimbledon title.

Keep It Clean

Jim Courier, one of the top-ranked players in the world, almost talked himself out of playing in the 1993 Wimbledon Championships. While playing against Jason Stoltenberg in the third round at Wimbledon that year, Courier disagreed with a line call and used such foul language that referee Alan Mills actually considered tossing Courier out of the tournament. When umpire Jeremy Shales took Jim Courier's side and told referee Mills he didn't consider Courier's verbal abuse bad enough to warrant a default, Alan Mills allowed Courier to continue to play. Jim Courier then went on to meet Pete Sampras in the finals, but lost.

The Bust Performance at Wimbledon

American Linda Siegel's performance at the 1979 Wimbledon tournament exposed Linda to the scrutiny of the crowd in a very embarrassing way. Linda, who at the time was a young 18-year-old tennis pro, wore an attractive but slightly low-cut halter for her match against tennis great Billie Jean King. Linda had to scramble around the court to keep up with Billie Jean's shots and during the hectic pace of the match one of Ms. Siegel's halter straps slipped down over her shoulder exposing part of Linda's upper body to view. Linda quickly covered up her bared chest and went on to lose the match to Billie Jean 6–1 and 6–3.

Birthday Wishes

Martina Navratilova and Boris Becker celebrated their birthdays in style in 1992. That year Navratilova won the Porsche Grand Prix in Frankfurt, Germany, on October 18, which was her birthday, and Becker won the ATP Tour World Championship, also in Frankfurt, Germany, on November 22, which was his birthday.

Net Result

John McEnroe, who is sometimes considered a bad boy of tennis, suffered a fall from grace during the 1980 Grand Prix Masters Tournament. McEnroe played Guillermo Vilas in an early round and, while chasing down a drop shot, tumbled over the net, knocked over a net judge, and also hit his head. However, the unexpected fall didn't hurt McEnroe, who returned after the accident to knock his foe out of the tournament.

Hot Topic

Scorching heat during the 1975 Wimbledon Tennis Tournament caused everyone on hand great discomfort and some embarrassment. Prim and proper English tennis fans were shocked and appalled when rising temperatures prompted the Duke of Kent to remove his jacket in a totally unacceptable display of Royal court manners.

Underlying Problem

Rosie Casals once found herself faced with an embarrassing problem while playing in the Virginia Slims Tennis Tournament in New York. Rosie forgot to pack underwear for her trip to the tournament and had none to wear under her tennis outfit. A member of the tournament staff had to rush out to a local store to purchase underwear so Rosie Casals could play her match.

Money Problems

It is not the custom for officials to present winners with real prize money at the conclusion of a tennis tournament. Normally winners receive symbolic empty envelopes at the tournament's award ceremony and are presented the actual checks at a later time. However, that wasn't the case at one Virginia Slims Tennis Championship won by Martina Navratilova. At the conclusion of the tournament Martina was handed an envelope which she thought was just symbolic so she tossed it away without ever opening it up. Imagine her shock later when she learned the envelope actually contained a check for her winnings. Luckily a quick search of a nearby trash can turned up the wayward envelope containing the missing prize money.

Snooze Alarm

Lineswoman Dorothy Cavis-Brown fell asleep at the 1964 Wimbledon Tennis Tournament during a match between Clark Graebner and Abe Segal.

A Handful

A very strange tennis match was played between Lita Liem of Indonesia and Marijka Schaar of the Netherlands at the 1972 Wimbledon Tournament. Both women were ambidextrous and continually changed their rackets from one hand to the other during play, neither utilizing a single backhand stroke between them the entire match!

Getting into Hot Water

Tracy Austin was favored to win the 1982 Avon Tennis Championship in Los Angeles until she was forced to drop out of the tournament for an unexpected reason. Boiling water was accidentally spilled on her a few days before the tournament began and she was unable to compete.

Quitting Time

Peter McNamara won the $142,000 Miracle Indoor Tennis Championship in 1981 when his foe, Vitas Gerulaitis, the defending champion, couldn't have his way. Gerulaitis got into an argument over a line call and demanded the removal of the referee and a service linesman. When officials refused to comply with Vitas' demands, Gerulaitis stubbornly sat down in his courtside chair and refused to play tennis until he got his way. At the time the score was 5–5 in the final set. Vitas Gerulaitis was issued a time warning and, when he ignored it, had two penalty points awarded against him. When Gerulaitis still refused to finish the match, the championship was awarded to Gerulaitis' opponent Peter McNamara. Vitas Gerulaitis was later fined for failing to complete a match and for abusing an official.

Forgetful

Even tennis pros can be forgetful. Once, at the Virginia Slims Tennis Tournament in New York, Jennifer Capriati forgot to bring her tennis outfit to the tournament and had to compete in a skirt and shirt borrowed from Steffi Graf.

Quick Change

Tennis pro Iile Nastase made his debut as a male stripper in 1979, performing his disrobing routine before fans at the U.S. Open Tennis Tournament. Nastase was playing Leo Palin in the first round when Iile decided that his tennis shorts were too sweaty to continue playing in. At a break in the action Nastase sent an attendant to fetch him a new pair of shorts. When the attendant arrived with the tennis shorts, Nastase quickly and unembarrassedly stripped off his sweaty shorts, while standing in full view of the grandstand, and then slipped on the dry ones.

The Butt of All Jokes

Sue Barker, a young and attractive tennis star from Britain during the 1970s and 1980s, had a keen sense of humor. She had two words printed on the back of a special undergarment she sometimes wore beneath her tennis skirt in those days. The words on the back of her underwear, she let it be known, were: "Smart Lass." Actually, the truth of the matter is that the second word on her backside did not contain the letter "L."

Going Courting

The fans who fill up the center court stands at the Wimbledon Tennis Tournament are usually prim and proper court buffs who behave with the utmost dignity during play. That's because the center court seats are usually reserved for the tournament's most distinguished guests. However, all of that changed in 1991 when heavy rains forced Wimbledon officials to reschedule play on the middle Sunday of the tourney, which is traditionally a day off. Due to the rescheduling, center court was opened up to ordinary fans for the first time in the history of Wimbledon, and the fans certainly appreciated the gesture of the All-England Club officials. They cheered, jeered, heckled, and even did the wave, much to the chagrin of tournament officials. After it was all over, the All-England Club officials vowed never to open the center court section to "common" fans again.

Curses, Foiled Again!

Who says talk is cheap? At the 1991 Wimbledon Tennis Championships, American tennis star John McEnroe was fined $1,000 for cursing out a linesman over a disputed call.

Plane Crazy

Sylvia Hanika won the $150,000 Monaco Women's Tennis Tournament in July of 1981 thanks to her opponent's tight travel schedule. Hanika was playing against Hana Mandlikova in the third set of the finals when Mandlikova called a sudden stop to play so she could catch a plane to Paris in order to play in another tournament.

Sylvia Hanika had won the first set and was leading in the third set when Hana Mandlikova called it quits and beat a hasty retreat to the airport. A rain delay of over an hour in the Monaco Tourney had apparently caused great scheduling problems for Mandlikova, who was booed loudly by fans who witnessed her hurried departure from the court.

Where's the Beef?

American tennis star John McEnroe was in Tokyo, Japan, to play in the Seiko Super Tournament in 1982. During his stay in Tokyo, McEnroe didn't like the taste of the beef served to him, so he had twelve steaks flown in especially for him from one of his favorite American restaurants, which was located in New York City.

Slap Shots

What a Streak!

Some people believe clothes make the man. Apparently, NHL goalie Gilles Gratton never agreed with that statement. When Gilles was a nine-year-old he stripped off his clothes and streaked through a baseball field at a Little League game when someone bet him a quarter he wouldn't do it.

Years later, as a professional hockey player in the minor leagues, Gratton repeated his bare-skin streak during a practice session with the Toronto Toros. On that occasion Gilles Gratton did wear some articles of clothing, namely socks and skates.

Gratton continued his revealing ways even after he made it into the National Hockey League in the 1970s. As a member of the Toronto Maple Leafs he once streaked around Mapleleaf Garden after practice, wearing only his skates and goalie pads!

If the Name Fits

The Quebec Nordiques of the NHL had a rookie goalie on their roster in 1993 whose last name was just perfect for an ice hockey player. The name of that ice hockey player was Garth Snow!

Unsettled Problem

Glenn Hall won or shared the Vezina Trophy, which is awarded to the NHL's top goalie, on three occasions. Hall captured the trophy in 1963 as a member of the Chicago Blackhawks and shared the trophy in 1967 with Chicago teammate Dennis Dejordy. He shared it again in 1969 as a member of the St. Louis Blues with fellow goalie Jacques Plante. Despite his great success as an NHL goalie, Glenn Hall was always very nervous before the start of a game. He was so jittery, in fact, that he got an upset stomach and always threw up in the locker room before the opening face-off.

Hit with a Suspension

Fans who watch NHL hockey know that to stay in the league most players have to be tough and know how to fight. In 1992 Montreal Canadiens winger Shayne Corson got suspended from his team . . . for getting involved in a fight in a bar during the season! Corson accepted the decision of the Canadiens' general manager, Serge Savard, and didn't try to fight it.

Fight Nice

Every hockey fan knows that "donnybrook" is hockey slang for a fight on the ice. Actually Donnybrook is a suburb of Dublin, Ireland, where an annual fair was held for more than 600 years. The fair was finally halted in 1855 because of the terrible brawls that always seemed to erupt at the town during the event. Those wild brawls are how donnybrook came to be known as a fight or brawl.

Cheaters Never Win

The Maine Mariners beat the Hershey (Pennsylvania) Bears in a minor league game in the American Hockey League during the 1979 season. The Mariners outscored the Bears 6–3, but ended up losing the contest when Hershey protested to the league president that Maine had used an ineligible player to ice the victory. The AHL president agreed and awarded the Hershey Bears a forfeit win over the Mariners. It was the first forfeit ever awarded in the long history of the AHL!

Talent Pool

The Pittsburgh Penguins won the Stanley Cup as the champions of the National Hockey League in 1990–91. The Penguins' success was largely due to the play of their super star scorer Mario Lemieux. To celebrate the team's big victory, Lemieux threw a wild party at his home in suburban Pittsburgh. At the bash, the Stanley Cup, the symbol of hockey supremacy, was put on display. Where did the coveted trophy end up before the night was over? It ended up underwater. Someone tossed the Stanley Cup into Mario Lemieux's swimming pool.

Penguin Power

When a bench-clearing brawl between teams from Germany and France broke out at the 1993 World Hockey Championships in Dortmund, Germany, Germany's mascot "Bully" did his duty. Bully, who was a guy wearing a penguin suit with skates and a stick, joined officials who tried to separate players from the two teams who were fighting on the ice. Unfortunately, the penguin peace patrol failed in its bid to calm the combatants and the brawl continued despite Bully's courageous but bizarre intervention.

Put in the Cooler

In August of 1988 forward Dino Ciccarelli of the Minnesota North Stars went to court and was sentenced to one day in jail and fined $1,000 for hitting the Toronto Maple Leafs' Luke Richardson with a stick during a game between Minnesota and Toronto in January of that year. It was the first time a hockey player was ever sentenced to the cooler for something he did on the ice.

Zip It

New York Ranger minor leaguer Dave Silk wasn't exactly relieved when he saw a police officer in the parking garage Silk had entered after leaving a nearby restaurant in 1980. The officer caught Silk emptying his bladder in a public place and arrested the former U.S. Olympic hockey star. The charges against Dave Silk were later dropped at the request of prosecutors, who felt the embarrassment of being arrested for urinating in a public place was punishment enough for a hockey celebrity.

Show Off

The best show on the ice at Maple Leaf Garden in Toronto during an NHL contest between the Maple Leafs and the St. Louis Blues on March 12, 1980, wasn't the hockey game. The event of the night was provided by a fan who jumped out on the ice wearing nothing but socks and skates. The nude fan skated around the rink for thirty seconds as police chased him and the crowd applauded. After the flashy skater was finally caught, he was arrested and charged with indecent exposure.

Flyer Flub

A once-in-a-lifetime hockey feat was accomplished by Philadelphia Flyer defenseman Garry Galley in a game against the Chicago Blackhawks on December 18, 1993. Galley scored a goal in a way that Flyers coach Terry Simpson had never seen before during his entire twenty-one years of coaching.

It all began with less than six minutes remaining in the second period of a game that was knotted at two goals each. The Flyers had control of the puck. Referee Kerry Fraser raised his arm to signal a delayed high sticking penalty against a Chicago player. As soon as a Blackhawk player touched the puck the whistle would blow to stop play and the penalty would be assessed.

Since the Flyers had the puck, Coach Terry Simpson called for the Flyers' goalie Tommy Soderstrom to exit his net so Philadelphia could get an extra attacker on the ice. Pulling the goalie under those circumstances was a normal procedure. An unguarded net was no liability since the whistle would stop play as soon as a Blackhawks player touched the puck. Unfortunately, no Chicago player had to touch the puck to chalk up a goal for the Blackhawks. As the Flyers' goalie skated off, Flyers defenseman Garry Galley accidentally shot the puck backwards into his own end and toward his team's unguarded net. Goalie Tommy Soderstrom saw the errant shot and tried to head off the puck, but couldn't catch up with it. Galley's shot went into the net for a Chicago goal. Chicago's Christian Ruutu, the last opposing player to touch the puck, was credited with the odd goal that Garry Galley had shot into his own net during a delayed penalty call.

Ticket Scalped

Goalie Fred Chittick of the Ottawa Capitals refused to show up for a playoff game against the Montreal Victorias in 1898. Chittick was so mad at the Ottawa management he never did play in the game. What was the reason for Chittick's anger? Fred felt the Ottawa management had not alloted him a fair share of complimentary tickets to the hockey contest.

L in New York

The New York Rangers played a fifty-game NHL schedule in 1943–44 and managed to post only six victories that season.

Best of the Worst

The Stanley Cup was won by the Chicago Blackhawks in 1937–38, making them the best team in the NHL. However, that season the Blackhawks didn't even post a winning record. Chicago won only 14 regular season games, lost 25 games, and tied 9 to finish third in the American Division.

That's Nothing

Frank Brimsek, who played for the Boston Bruins and won the Vezina Trophy as the NHL's best goaltender in 1939 and 1942, had a nickname that was flattering at the time he played, but is not today. Frank Brimsek was known as "Mr. Zero."

Bad Debut

John Muckler's debut as the coach of the Buffalo Sabres in 1991 wasn't exactly lucky. Buffalo lost to the Hartford Whalers by the score of 8–4. In a way Muckler's opening night behind the bench for the Sabres may have been doomed to defeat from the start. John Muckler's first night as head coach of the Buffalo Sabres was on Friday the 13th!

Better Daze

The Buffalo Sabres were in Quebec City in April of 1992 to take on the Quebec Nordiques in an NHL game. During the contest a Nordiques fan leaped out into the rink and challenged players sitting on the Buffalo bench to a fight. The Sabres were up to the challenge and pummeled the guy, who'd issued the challenge just to win a bet with a friend. The fan won the bet, but lost the fight.

Bizarre Baseball

Heads-up Player

Slugger Jose Canseco of the American League's Texas Rangers has a reputation for being a heads-up player. Canseco, who shared the 1991 AL Home Run Crown with Cecil Fielder of the Detroit Tigers (44 round-trippers each), knows a lot of ways to turn an ordinary pitched ball into a fence-clearing four-sacker. On May 26, 1993, while playing the Indians at Cleveland's home field, Jose found a unique new way to turn a pitch into a homer. He just used his head.

Unfortunately, the way he used it helped the Indians' Carlos Martinez turn his routine fly ball to right field into a Big League dinger.

Here's how it happened. In the fourth inning Canseco was roaming right field for Texas as Martinez led off for the tribe. Carlos smacked a deep fly ball to right, which Jose easily circled under at the warning track. It looked like a routine play until Canseco suddenly turned his head as he approached the outfield wall. Martinez's hit grazed past Canseco's glove, konked him right on the head, and bounced up over the wall and into the stands for a home run. Even Jose Canseco had to laugh as Carlos Martinez broke into a home run trot as he rounded first base. It was one of those rare times in baseball when a player who made a heads-up play ended up looking silly. To add insult to injury, the Indians beat the Rangers in that contest 7–6.

Up and Down

In July of 1953 Dick Teed of the Brooklyn Dodgers was summoned up from the minor leagues to join "the show," which is what professional players call the major leagues. Teed became the Dodgers' number-two catcher behind Roy Campanella when regular Dodger reserve backstop Rube Walker was injured. After spending six years in the minors, Teed was thrilled to finally get a chance to

75

bat in the major leagues. Teed's chance to swing the lumber against a big league hurler finally came when he pinch-hit for Jim Hughes, a Brooklyn relief pitcher, in a game against the Milwaukee Braves. Teed faced pitcher Max Furkont. Using a bat borrowed from Dodger star Carl Furillo, Dick Teed promptly struck out in his major league debut at the plate. That one strikeout was Dick Teed's only major league at bat, as he was returned to the minor leagues shortly afterward and never played in the majors again. However, Dick remained in baseball and became a big league scout.

Chicken Cooped Up

Second baseman Delino DeShields of the Montreal Expos missed playing some big league games in April of 1993 because he chickened out when he felt ill. DeShields came down with a case of the chicken pox and was lost to the Expos for several games.

Gate Crasher

Outfielder Rodney McCray of the Vancouver Canadians of the Pacific Coast League truly became a high-impact player in the 1991 season. That year McCray crashed right through a fence in left field while trying to snare a well-hit fly ball.

Cold Logic

Baseball might well be a young man's game. Former All-Star catcher Carlton Fisk was a 43-year-old major leaguer in 1991. After Fisk was required to play ball on a chilly 40-degree night in April that season, he quipped, "I don't think I should be asked to play when the temperature drops below my age."

Hitting the Jackpot

Baseball star Pete Rose sold the bat he used to collect hit number 4,192 that broke Ty Cobb's hit record. Rose collected $129,000 for the bat, which he sold to insurance agent Steve Wolter.

Mound Misery

Pitcher Anthony Young of the New York Mets suffered through a year of miserable luck on the mound in 1993 even though the young Met hurler turned in record-breaking performances that season. To Young's chagrin the records he set that year were for pitching futilely. It all began on May 6, 1992, when the Mets lost to the Cincinnati Reds and hurler Anthony Young was charged with the defeat. That loss started a disastrous domino effect for Young, who chalked up loss after loss on the mound until he had a string of 19 straight losing appearances by June of 1993. Those 19 consecutive losses tied Anthony with the Mets' Craig Anderson, who had established the Mets team record for the longest losing streak by a pitcher which he set between 1962 and 1964.

When Young took the mound on June 9, 1993, he was looking to snap his losing skid against the Chicago Cubs. A win was not in the cards that day for the hurler, as the Mets lost and Young set a new team mark for consecutive mound losses by dropping his 20th straight contest.

Unfortunately, Young's mound misery didn't end there. On June 22, 1993, Anthony lost his 23rd straight game, as the Montreal Expos defeated Young and his Met teammates. Anthony Young's 23rd straight loss tied the major league baseball record of 23 consecutive mound failures by a pitcher, set by the Boston Braves' Cliff Curtis way back in 1910–11.

Still Anthony Young continued to pitch for the Mets and still he continued to set records for losing. On June 27, 1993, Young set a new low mark for major league hurlers when he was saddled with his 24th straight loss, which came at the hands of the St. Louis Cardinals. The unlucky Met right-hander didn't give up and kept pitching his way into the record books by losing.

Finally on July 24, 1993, after going down to defeat an astounding record of 27 straight times, pitcher Anthony Young won a baseball game. On that date, Young and the Mets topped the Florida Marlins to end the longest consecutive losing streak by a pitcher in major league history.

Whoa, Snow?

A freak winter storm on April 6, 1982, dumped huge amounts of snow and brought sub-freezing temperatures to the Midwest and Northeast causing the unexpected postponement of opening-day baseball games in the American League cities of Detroit, Chicago, Cleveland, Milwaukee, and New York, and the National League cities of Philadelphia and Pittsburgh.

Champion Breakfast

In 1993 a cereal box from 1951 with a picture of St. Louis Cardinal slugger Stan Musial on it was sold at auction in New York city for $1,210. Saving box tops used to be profitable. Today, apparently, it's wise to save the entire box.

Not a Hothead

In the early days of baseball, way before air-conditioned dugouts, New York Yankee star Babe Ruth had a weird way of keeping his cool during ball games played under a blazing sun. The ingenious Babe would wear wet cabbage leafs under his cap to keep a cool head.

Production Line

Playing outfield for the New York Mets in 1962 were Richie Ashburn, Gus Bell, and Frank Thomas. Mets manager Casey Stengel felt his outfield group would certainly contribute to his team's success that season. Ashburn, Bell, and Thomas were all married men with large families and Casey thought players with lots of kids were a good sign of things to come. "If my outfield produces as well on the field as it does off the field," quipped the crafty Met mentor to reporters at the start of the season, "we'll win the pennant." Of course, the Mets didn't win the pennant that year.

Throwing the Bull

Baseball player Dave Kingman was best known for hitting mammoth home runs, but he also had a cannon arm that could fire long-range baseball bombs. Chicago Cub infielder Larry Biittner once told reporters he saw his teammate Kingman make an astounding toss from left field while playing at the Houston Astrodome. Biittner claimed Kingman fired a ball from left field that sailed into the third-base dugout, bounced down some steps, bounded up a runway, and finally came to rest in a bathroom toilet.

Mitt to be Tied

Some modern professional athletes wear white shoes so they'll stand out. When Babe Ruth was playing baseball he occasionally used a special white baseball mitt.

Bats!

Talk about beaning the opposition. On May 7, 1991, the St. Louis Cardinals travelled to Atlanta to take on the Atlanta Braves. During the game the Braves' Mike Heath went down swinging at the plate in the second inning and lost his grip on the bat. As Heath swung for strike three the bat flew out of his hands and into the stands where it hit a female fan on the head. Luckily the woman wasn't injured. Just who did Heath accidentally konk with his bat? The woman was Mrs. Joe Torre, the wife of St. Louis Cardinals manager Joe Torre.

Scrambled Fans

Joe Carter of the Toronto Blue Jays hit a home run in the bottom of the ninth inning in the sixth game of the 1993 World Series to win baseball's coveted championship crown for Toronto. The losers in the 1993 World Series were the Philadelphia Phillies, and the Phillies hurler who served up that home-run pitch to Carter was reliever Mitch Williams.

Just hours after Williams gave up that series-winning four-sacker to the opposition, some thirty teenage fans showed how they felt about Williams' pitching performance by driving to the house used by the Phillies' pitcher in Moorestown, New Jersey. When the teens arrived at Williams' home they served up some sloppy pitches of their own by firing dozens of raw eggs at Mitch's home sweet home. Williams, however, wasn't in the house at the time.

Soaked at Home

A major league baseball game was played first outdoors and then indoors at the same stadium for the first time in history on June 7, 1989. When dark clouds formed and posed a threat of rain over the Toronto Skydome during a game between the Milwaukee Brewers and the Toronto Blue Jays, the stadium's retractable roof, which had been open at the start of the game, closed up, making the outdoor stadium a weatherproof indoor stadium; and the game went on. Unfortunately, the roof didn't close quickly enough for home plate umpire Rich Garcia. He got rained on and soaked before the stadium's roof sealed completely.

Cub Bares All

Marla Collins worked as a ballgirl for the Chicago Cubs from 1982 until 1986. She was released from her job with the Chicago team in July of 1986 just days before an issue of *Playboy* magazine hit the stands containing photos of the Cubs ballgirl, who had decided to bare it all. Even though the nude photos of Marla were admittedly tastefully done, the Chicago Cubs organization did not authorize, condone, or approve of the appearance of one of their employees in *Playboy* and so Marla and the Cubs parted company.

Clothes Call at the Plate

When Daryl Spencer's baseball career with the San Francisco Giants ended he travelled to Japan to play professionally with the Hankyu Braves. Spencer didn't always see eye to eye with Yukio Nishimoto, the manager of the Japanese team Spencer was on. Once, Nishimoto benched Spencer because he didn't think the American ballplayer could get a hit off the opposing team's pitcher. Since Spencer had a batting average of .340 against that particular pitcher, an angered Daryl decided to get even with his manager. Spencer took his time changing as the locker room emptied. When he heard the stadium's public address announcer call out the names of the home team starters, Spencer made his move. Wearing only his underwear and shower clogs, Daryl Spencer picked up a bat and walked out onto the field of the Japanese stadium. Spencer made a grand entrance in front of the startled crowd and then slowly strolled over to the on-deck circle. Daryl calmly took several practice swings before he was ordered off the field. Daryl Spencer was fined and suspended for his strange batting exhibition, but he didn't care because he felt he'd evened the score with his Japanese manager.

Dream Player

Pitcher Steve McCatty of the Chicago White Sox had sleep trouble in September of 1982. McCatty peacefully overslept when he was supposed to be at Chicago's Comisky Park warming up for a game he was scheduled to pitch. Chicago manager Billy Martin replaced McCatty's name in the lineup and later made Steve's untimely dream seem like a nightmare when he chewed out the hurler for being in bed when he should have been in the ballpark.

A Big Smeller

In 1992 the South Atlantic League baseball franchise in Albany, Georgia, was a team called the Albany Polecats. In case you don't know, polecat is another word for skunk.

Getting Fanned

In the blink of an umpire's eye, the Boston Red Sox won and then lost a game to the New York Yankees on September 18, 1993, thanks to the bizarre behavior of two teenage fans at Yankee Stadium. The Sox had victory within their grasp as they held a 3 to 1 lead over the Yanks with two outs in the bottom of the ninth inning. One more out would retire the home team Bronx Bombers. That out appeared to be a sure thing when Yankee hitter Mike Stanley lofted an easy fly ball to Boston left-fielder Mike Greenwell with New York runner Mike Gallego on first base. But the win was not to be for Boston.

Just before the Boston pitcher delivered the ball, two teenage fans jumped out of the stands along third base and dashed out onto the playing field. Instantly, home plate umpire Drew Coble called time-out, even though Sox hurler Greg Harris was already into his motion. Harris didn't hear the umpire's call and neither did the catcher, the batter, or hardly anyone else. The pitcher pitched. The batter hit the ball. And the outfielder caught it.

Boston thought the game was over, as security personnel captured the two overzealous fans and escorted them from the field. The umpire ruled that the game was not over, that Stanley's third fly-out was officially "no pitch." No pitch meant Stanley was still up, so the game was not over. Despite protests from Boston manager Butch Hobson, the easy out that should have ended the game had to be replayed. Mike Stanley got another life at the plate and took advantage of it. After the apparent game-ending out was ruled "no play," Mike Stanley singled to left field. The Yankees then went on to rally for three runs and escaped with a bizarre 4–3 victory instead of a 3–1 loss. Truly it was a victory the Yankees owed to their fans.

Rockies Woes

The Colorado Rockies had two home baseball contests snowed out in 1993, their inaugural year of play. The first snowout took place in Denver on April 12, 1993, against the New York Mets, and the second was on September 13, 1993, against the Houston Astros.

Run Down

When pitcher Charlie Hough of the Florida Marlins scored a run in a game on May 12, 1993, it was a special occasion. It was the first run Hough had scored in a major league game since 1979, when he was a member of the Los Angeles Dodgers.

Repeat Performance

Pitcher Urban Shocker hurled his St. Louis Browns team to a complete game 6–2 victory over the Chicago White Sox in the first game of a doubleheader on September 6, 1924. Then, to the dismay of the White Sox, Urban took the mound again for the second game of the contest and notched an identical 6–2 complete game win over Chicago.

Ouch Rule

Many baseball rules have changed over the years to improve the game. One funny rule change improved the health prospects of umpires. In the very early days of baseball, any thrown ball that hit an umpire was officially ruled a "take-it-over" situation. The rule meant that, if a batter hit a ball and the player who fielded it hit an umpire with his throw, the batter would have to do the whole thing over. Wily infielders who found themselves having to field tough plays began to use the rule to their advantage. When they fielded a ball and had no chance to throw out the batter who hit it, they just threw the ball at an umpire instead. When the ball hit the umpire, the batter had to return to home plate for a do-over even though he was safe. The rule was changed so that when a ball hit an umpire it remained in play. After the rule change, fielders stopped intentionally hitting umpires with their throws on tough plays.

She Knew

When California Angels pitcher Bert Blyleven first returned to action in May of 1992 after missing two seasons due to an injury, he wasn't sure he could notch his 280th career win against the Cleveland Indians. Patty Blyleven, however, had no doubts that her hubby would be successful in his return to the mound after his long absence. She sent him 280 roses and handed out "Welcome Back, Bert" T-shirts to his Angels teammates all before the game on May 31, 1992. Patty sure knew what Bert would do when the game began. Bert Blyleven beat the Indians 3–1 to record his 280th career win even though he hadn't pitched in two seasons.

Bat Outmanned

When the Pittsburgh Pirates held Bat Day at their home stadium in 1979, a fan with bats in his belfry found a frightening use for the souvenir bat he received upon admission to the stands. During the final inning of the Pirates' 5–0 loss to the Cubs, the fan let his bat fly in the direction of Pittsburgh right-fielder Dave Parker, missing the superstar by some thirty feet. The bat thrower was identified by security personnel and later turned over to the Pittsburgh police.

Bell Belle

When sports reporter Allison Gordon of the *Toronto Star* entered the Toronto Blue Jays locker room in 1980 to do an interview, she used a unique warning system to alert any players who weren't properly clothed that she was on her way. Gordon used a small bell presented to her by Barry Bonnell, an outfielder on the 1980 Toronto Blue Jays squad.

Rain Pain

The Houston Astros play baseball in the Houston Astrodome, an enclosed stadium that is guaranteed to be weatherproof. Amazing as it sounds, a baseball game between the Astros and the Pittsburgh Pirates was rained out in Houston on June 15, 1976. A fluke cloud-burst dumped ten inches of rain on the city on that date and, even though the field stayed dry, umpires, fans, and stadium personnel were unable to travel through the rain to reach the Astrodome, so the game had to be cancelled.

Picture Imperfect

The Red Sox's team picture for the 1980 season was missing two of the club's top stars. Future Hall-of-Famer Carl Yastrzemski was absent from the picture because he didn't arrive at Boston's Fenway Park on time for the photo shoot. Yastrzemski was tardy because he was at a baseball game out of town watching his son, Carl Jr., play. All-Star Jim Rice wasn't in the photo either because he overslept and slumbered through the event.

A Lot of Flies

When the Texas Rangers played the Kansas City Royals at Royals Stadium on the night of September 2, 1992, the game featured high flies, pop flies, and swarms of pesky houseflies. In the third inning of the contest a huge cloud of midges, relatives of the housefly, descended on the stadium. Many fans in the lower levels of the stadium were pestered so much by attacking bugs that they were forced to flee from their seats. Out on the field, players from both teams were tormented by the tiny invaders but the game continued despite the insect onslaught. A biology professor, asked later about the insect invasion, explained that the normal breeding pattern of the bugs had been disturbed by heavy rains that year and the insects were probably attracted to the stadium by its lights.

Wrong Number

Fans of Yankee baseball were surprised when they looked at the numbers posted on the scoreboard to see who was playing third base for the Yanks' home game on August 6, 1980. According to the scoreboard, number 4 was scheduled to play the hot corner. Seeing that number certainly excited everyone in the stands, because number 4 belonged to deceased Yankee immortal Lou Gehrig and had been retired many years ago. Gehrig didn't play in the game, however. Somebody goofed when they set up the scoreboard and accidentally inserted Lou's number 4 instead of Aurelio Rodriguez's number 27.

Singles Not Barred

On June 18, 1993, the Detroit Tigers held a special promotion at Tiger Stadium. The promotion was called "Singles Night" and the Tiger team celebrated the promotion by getting fifteen hits, all of them singles, in their game against the Toronto Blue Jays.

A Lot of Bull

In June of 1993 the Durham (North Carolina) Bulls minor league team wanted to honor former Bulls second baseman Joe Morgan, who played many years in the major leagues and was elected to Baseball's Hall of Fame. To honor Joe Morgan the Bulls retired uniform number 18, which they believed Joe had worn during the three months Morgan had spent on the Durham squad in 1963. A day after good old number 18 was retired as a tribute to Joe Morgan, a longtime Durham Bulls fan produced a roster of the 1963 Bulls team that showed Joe Morgan had actually worn uniform number 8 as a Bulls player. The Durham Bulls had made a mistake and accidentally retired the wrong number. Number 18 had actually been worn by an infielder named Tommy Murray in 1963.

A Yellow Streak

The Brooklyn Dodgers and the St. Louis Cardinals used a yellow baseball as an experiment in the first game of their doubleheader on August 2, 1938. Obviously the experiment was a big failure.

Gone in a Flash

Former New York Met and Yankee outfielder Ron Swoboda was working as a radio sports announcer at a Milwaukee radio station in December of 1980 when he closed out his broadcast with a late-breaking story. Swoboda told his listeners that his contract at the station had not been renewed and he wanted to be the first to break the news of his termination.

Blind Spot

Chicago Cubs outfielder Andre Dawson was fined $1,000 for arguing over a strike called by umpire Joe West in 1991. When he paid the fine by check, Dawson finally had the last word in the dispute. On the memo line of the check he wrote, "Donation for the blind."

Flagged Down

The 1992 World Series was played between the Atlanta Braves of the United States and the Toronto Blue Jays of Canada. During a pregame presentation of the countries' flags at a World Series game in Atlanta, an Atlanta-based U.S. Marine Corps Color Guard accidentally hung the Canadian flag upside down as the National Anthems of Canada and the United States were played. Toronto got even for the mistake by winning the World Series that year.

Age Outrage

Four-year-old Kyle Carnaroli almost made baseball history in August of 1993 by becoming the youngest person to ever play in a professional baseball game. Playing outfield for an inning for the Pocatello Posse, a minor league team in Idaho, was supposed to be Kyle's prize for winning a contest in which contestants vied to name Pocatello's new entry in the Pioneer League. The pint-sized Pocatello Posse player was issued a uniform and was set to man right field for his team in a game against the Medicine Hat Blue Jays when the National Association of Professional Baseball Leagues stepped in. Association officials advised the general manager of the Pocatello Posse that their three-foot six-inch, fifty-pound right fielder was ineligible, as a safety precaution, to play minor league baseball. To make good on the prize promotion, Kyle Carnaroli got to trot out to right field for the playing of the National Anthem and then he returned to the Posse bench to watch the game from there. He didn't mind not actually playing

School Daze

Somerset Vo Tech's baseball team didn't have much luck on the diamond during the early 1990s. The New Jersey high school squad lost 57 straight games before breaking its long losing streak with a victory on May 7, 1993.

Dark Daze

Slugger Sid Bream had a chance to put his Atlanta Braves team ahead of the Philadelphia Phillies in a game played at Atlanta-Fulton County Stadium on August 5, 1993. The Braves were losing 5–4. Bream was at the plate with one out and the bases loaded when the lights literally went out in Georgia. Six banks of stadium lights suddenly blacked out, causing the game to be delayed for fifteen minutes. The delay certainly didn't help Sid or the Braves. When the lights came back on and play resumed, an impatient Bream swung and hit into a double play to end the Braves' scoring threat. Atlanta also lost the game 10–4 to Philadelphia.

Plate Fate

New York Mets pitcher Randy Tate went 0 for 41 at the plate in 1975, while Chicago Cubs pitcher Bob Buhl demonstrated his despicable batting ability in 1962 by going 0 for 70.

Top Flop

Manager Eddie Sawyer of the Philadelphia Phillies only made one trip to the World Series as a skipper during his career. In 1950 he took the Phillies to the title tilt and lost four straight games to the New York Yankees, who captured the crown without allowing Sawyer to record a single World Series victory. Eddie Sawyer's claim to fame is that he lost every World Series game he ever managed.

Family Feud

The family that plays baseball together often stays together even if it means getting tossed out of a major league baseball game together. That's exactly what happened when the San Francisco Giants played the Colorado Rockies at Denver on May 12, 1993. After the two teams got involved in a bench-clearing brawl, Giants hitting coach Bobby Bonds was ejected from the game and so was Bonds' son, Giants player Barry Bonds. San Francisco did beat Colorado 8–2 in the contest despite the absence of the battling Bonds family.

Spit Fit

In 1980 Atlanta Braves manager Bobby Cox was suspended for three games by National League President Chub Feeney for spitting tobacco juice on umpire Jerry Dale during an argument in a game against the Los Angeles Dodgers.

Busch League

New York Mets pitcher Tom Hausman drove his station wagon to Busch Stadium for a Mets game against the St. Louis Cardinals in 1979. Hausman parked his car in a Busch Stadium garage and went into the stadium to pitch for his team. While Tom Hausman was busy on the mound for the Mets, thieves in the garage were busy breaking into his car. Crooks stole a color television set, a tape player, and men's and women's clothing from Tom Hausman's station wagon.

Bottoms Up

When the New York Yankees travelled to Chicago to play the White Sox in 1979 they got an eyeful of the home team's fans, or is that fannies? Every night after the Yanks finished playing the Sox during the three-game stand, a young woman fan bared her fanny in front of the New York Yankees team bus before it left the stadium. Reporters photographed the event as proof that it occurred, but no one could prove a startling rumor that later surfaced. Rumor had it that some members of the 1979 Yankee team had actually autographed the fan's bare backside.

Lightning Strikes Three

Pitcher Ryan Whitaker of the University of Arkansas was on the Arkansas baseball diamond prior to a college baseball contest against the University of Georgia when lightning struck. A bolt of lightning hit the college stadium scoreboard knocking Whitaker to the ground. Ryan was rushed to a nearby hospital but wasn't injured. In fact, after being knocked down by lightning he returned to the field to pitch two scoreless innings against Georgia, which helped his Arkansas team to a 5–4 victory.

Index

About the Author

Michael Joseph Pellowski was an All-Star high school player in two sports in New Jersey in the 1960s and attended Rutgers College on an athletic scholarship. At Rutgers he earned seven letters in football and baseball. In football he captained the defensive squad in 1970 and earned Honorable Mention A.P. and E.C.A.C. All-East honors. In baseball he posted a .314 career batting average and once had six consecutive pinch hits. After college he had professional football trials in Canada (Montreal) and the NFL (New England) and played semi-professionally in the Atlantic Coast Football League (Hartford, Conn.) and the Eastern Football League (Plainfield, N.J.). He also coached high school sports in New Jersey before turning to writing sports books and books for young readers in the 1970s. He has penned numerous books.